The Three of Them Were Talking,

and the whole mad episode began.

"This is the third year she's refused the Men's Club's invitation to be your partner at their annual ball," Henry told Joe.

"There's something about the Mulholland name..." Francine began.

Joe protested. "She doesn't know me. How could she be prejudiced against me? This could be solved if I could just be with her for a while. I thought we had her boxed in at the tennis tournament, and she actually vanished into thin air. How'd she do that?"

Francine shrugged, thinking, frowning, before she said musingly, "If you really think you just need some time with Peggy, I believe I have an idea...."

Dear Reader,

Welcome to Silhouette! Our goal is to give you hours of unbeatable reading pleasure, and we hope you'll enjoy each month's six new Silhouette Desires. These sensual, provocative love stories are both believable and compelling—sometimes they're poignant, sometimes humorous, but always enjoyable.

Indulge yourself. Experience all the passion and excitement of falling in love along with our heroine as she meets the irresistible man of her dreams and together they overcome all obstacles in the path to a happy ending.

If this is your first Desire, I hope it'll be the first of many. If you're already a Silhouette Desire reader, thanks for your support! Look for some of your favorite authors in the coming months: Stephanie James, Diana Palmer, Dixie Browning, Ann Major and Doreen Owens Malek, to name just a few.

Happy reading!

Isabel Swift
Senior Editor

SDRL-7/85

LASS SMALL
Tangled Web

Silhouette Desire

Published by Silhouette Books New York

America's Publisher of Contemporary Romance

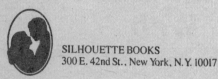

SILHOUETTE BOOKS
300 E. 42nd St., New York, N.Y. 10017

Copyright © 1985 by Lass Small

Distributed by Pocket Books

ISBN: 0-373-05241-3

First Silhouette Books printing November 1985

10 9 8 7 6 5 4 3 2 1

America's Publisher of Contemporary Romance

Printed in the U.S.A.

LASS SMALL

started writing after attending a workshop where she received the following advice: "If you want to start writing, start." She did, and she's never looked back. In fact, she says, "I *love* writing. I love all aspects of it." When she's not writing the novels that have made her popular, she likes to spend her time reading, swimming and enjoying life with her husband and four children.

To Texas
The Largest State in the Union

(...when the greenhouse effect
takes place and Alaska melts)

Prologue

The whole mad episode began when the three of them met at Francine's apartment, sitting in her living room on a hot, August day in San Antonio, and Joe said again, "It would be solved if I could just be with her for a while."

Henry grinned. "That Mulholland charm?"

"Now, Henry, you know women go wild over Joe."

"Francine..." Joe moved in impatient protest at her words.

"This is the third year she's refused the Men's Club's invitation to their annual ball as your partner." Henry smiled as he pointed out that germane fact. "That ought to clue you in that she's just not interested."

"There's something about the Mulholland name..." Francine began.

Joe protested, "She doesn't know me. How could she be prejudiced against me?"

Francine shook her head slowly. "But she is. How many times now have I cleverly set up an 'accidental' meeting and Peggy smelled a rat?"

"Rat?" Henry repeated with pardonable humor.

The other two plotters ignored him and Joe said, "I thought we had her boxed in at the tennis tournament, and she actually vanished into thin air. How'd she do that?"

Francine shrugged, thinking, frowning, before she asked Joe, "Do you really think you just need some time with her?"

"I do. I need the chance with her."

There was a brief silence, then Francine said musingly, "I believe I have an idea...."

One

Just before lunch, as directed, Margaret Indiana Dillon walked straight across the lobby toward the elevators of the Hilton, on the river in downtown San Antonio. Margaret was her formal name, but she was called Peggy.

She was wearing a discreet navy-blue summer suit, and as requested, she carried a wide-brimmed, cream straw hat. She walked slowly, looking around, and she tried to keep her mouth from thinning out in temper. Francine was the outside of too much.

"Peggy," Francine had said on the phone that morning. "Henry has me boxed in down here. He's off to God-only-knows which oil well, and he expects me to sit here and wait for him to show up. I will not!"

"Then leave," Peggy had told her with the logic of the uninvolved. "You're a grown woman. Walk right on out of there."

"Yeah, and one of his buddies downstairs will follow me."

"So?"

"I don't want to be followed. They'd go along and watch out for me and report in to Henry, and he'd know exactly where I was and what I was doing."

"I thought you liked him." Peggy had frowned into the phone.

"Oh, I do. But I like *him*. I want him to think about me and *wonder* where I am and who I'm with."

"Now, Francine, that's childish."

"So I'm not all grown up and mature like you, acting twenty-two. I don't want to sit here, and I don't want to be followed by a hovering bunch of old buddies who have all the time in the world and are bored, so they find doing this little favor for Henry more interesting than the stock market while it's too hot for polo."

"Francine..."

"I have a plan...." And that's when Francine laid it all out, and now here was Margaret Indiana Dillon, dressing in a navy-blue suit, carrying a large-brimmed straw hat as she walked across the lobby of the Hilton in a fine temper for giving in—again—to one of Francine's idiotic schemes.

It was their mothers' faults. The two had married men from Indiana who, after graduating from West Point, had been assigned to Fort Sam Houston at San Antonio. With seven army fields around the city, a great many new officers married San Antonio girls, and that's why the city is called the Mother-in-law of the Army. And when army careers are completed, a good many of the families retire there.

After hearing so much about Indiana, Francine's and Peggy's mothers chose Indiana as a middle name for their daughters and, with them only two days apart in age, sentimentally ruled that the unrelated girls were twins.

It's all very well and good for parents to decide children should be close, but it can be a burden to the offspring, who often have nothing in common but parents who have committed them to being friends. And Francine involved Peggy in endless schemes.

There in the Hilton Peggy gave the lobby mirror a cool, disgruntled glance and thought how different she and Francine looked. She was tall, blond and slight, while Francine was a tall, gorgeous brunette. This deception would never work.

She took a quick scan of the entrances to see if she could spot any of the lurking good-old-boys who were supposed to be guarding Francine, but Peggy could see no one suspicious. Either the guards were more subtle than Peggy supposed—who would really do such a mindless, silly errand for Henry?—or Francine's imagination was running more rampant than it usually did.

The call button on the elevator was a heat sensor and only needed the hint of a warm finger, but in her temper Peggy punched it anyway, and then stood seething because she had been so stupid as to have entered again into some dumb episode with Francine. How could she allow this to happen?

People slowly collected around Peggy, waiting for the elevator, and Peggy idly noted the variety in dress. Anything was acceptable, from the perfectly fitted two-thousand-dollar suit over there to those soft, deceptively casual denims that were worn and faded—and graced the gorgeous body of a man who was too near for her to glance up at his face. She was tempted to study him, but she had learned long ago that no woman did that without risking the impression that she was flirting. And Peggy did not flirt.

When they entered the elevator, Denims stayed at her shoulder. He was probably older, for he politely removed his Stetson, so in the brief moment when she could have peeked at him, the hat blocked her view.

She became quickly aware of a strange, magnetic pull from his masculine body to her feminine one, and she was a little amused by that. Most likely he was a tobacco-chewing, rough-tongued semi-hermit who hated women.

He was probably a sheep-man. Her mother's people had been cattlemen a few generations back, and the family had inherited a dislike of sheep so strong that by now it was probably genetic. None of her family had ever even tasted lamb.

He didn't smell of sheep or horse or tobacco. He smelled of sunshine, wind, freedom and open places. And she wondered if he too felt the strange attraction that she felt.

When she came to Francine's floor, she stepped off—and old Denims followed her! That did give her pause. Had she led them to Francine? She hesitated, still not looking right at him, but he turned the other way and strode off with purpose. He knew where he was going and was not at all attracted to her. He probably hadn't even seen her. Perhaps she had absorbed some of Francine's imagination through osmosis? Good grief.

Before Peggy knocked on Francine's door, she had to stop for a minute in order to remember the code tap Francine had insisted she use. Two quick raps and a pause before the third one. Francine jerked open the door, snatched her inside, shot a look both ways down the hall, then popped back inside to slam the door and lean against it. "Did anyone follow you?"

She was in attractive disarray, her brunette hair disturbed by restless fingers and her lovely body clad in a simply gorgeous pale silk kimono.

Peggy frowned at her. "Are you afraid of Henry?"

"Of course not! Don't be ridiculous! Did you see anyone?"

"No. Listen, Fran. Henry has always seemed a nice enough man, but you make me very nervous with all this dash-and-hide business. What are you doing? Is there something about Henry I ought to know?"

"It's just that he stakes me out and then leaves me." Francine pushed tired hands through her hair and let her arms drop down in something of a snit. "I want to be courted. I want him to care about me and come to see me and call me and quit just having me...reserved."

"Do you want to go out with other men? Is that it?"

"No, no, no, *no*. I love Henry."

"Are you trying to make him jealous? I don't understand you. Why are you here in a hotel room? You have an apartment in town."

"It's part of the confusion." Francine appeared logical.

"You're not being held captive. Apparently he just wants someone to watch out for you. Right?"

"Yes. But it isn't *him*. I want *him*."

"Francine." Peggy's tone was exasperated as she walked over and sat down on the sofa, then looked at her "twin." "I really don't understand you at all."

"You don't have to," Francine said calmly. "Only Henry must."

"He's a busy man. He works hard. His businesses are scattered. His interests are diversified. He has to keep in touch with all of them. He doesn't have time to dance attendance. And, Francine, if you should marry him, it wouldn't change. This is the way it will be. Have you thought of that? This is the real man. He's not fooling you about it. This *is* how it would be. If you can't handle it now, you'd be divorced in a year if you married him."

"I have to know that he wants only me, not a convenient woman. And that he's not getting married because he thinks now is a good time and I look good. That I'll stick around waiting for him to show up."

Peggy studied Francine, suspecting for the first time that there might be a solid person under all that fluff. "When you two are together..."

"It's heaven." Francine gave her a steady look.

Peggy threw up her hands in surrender. "Tell me what to do."

"There are times when I think our mothers were smart to make us 'twins.'"

"I'm two days older. Never forget that," Peggy said sourly.

"Give me your suit and hat; you'll wear mine." Francine gestured to the poisonous purple suit lying on the bed.

"You're kidding! *That*?"

"It's attention-getting," Francine explained impatiently. "I wore it in here, and they all saw me in it. They'll see you leave wearing it, and they'll think you're me. Brilliant, huh?"

"I don't think I can wear it even across the lobby without throwing up. Where on earth did you get it?" Peggy frowned at the suit lying there hideously.

"Wear sunglasses," Francine immediately advised, then added brightly, "it'll help the deception!"

"De-ception?" Peggy repeated the word, drawing it out. "You do know about the tangled webs woven by deception?"

"I'm not deceiving Henry."

Peggy sighed. "Well, do I wear a scarf? My hair..."

"Put your hair up and wear this hat." Francine lifted a garish yellow, floppy-brimmed hat from the dresser.

"My God!" Peggy gasped in awe. "That...with..." She couldn't finish the sentence but pointed to the purple suit, and her face must have turned a yellow-green.

"It's not for long," Francine snapped impatiently. "You can do this for me. My car is right out in front. I've called down, and it'll be waiting."

"And your car is..." Peggy said faintly.

"...Red." Francine finished her sentence.

"Red." Peggy echoed with a nod. "With that bilious purple and that sickening yellow."

"You won't have to wear it for very long," Francine repeated in a comforting way. "Only until just after they catch you and find out you're not me."

"Catch me?"

"Of course! What did you think this whole exercise is all about? You'll lure them away and they'll follow you. They'll jump into their pickup trucks and tail you right out of town. You take Highway 16 toward Freer. There's a truck stop down the road a piece. You can drive in there, go inside and they'll follow you like motherless ducks. You sit down and toy with your tea and finally you take off your hat!" Francine finished dramatically.

"I have to keep it on until then?"

"Of course! It'll hide your hair and most of your face. You have a nicer nose than mine."

Peggy gave Francine a slow look that said compliments weren't appropriate. "So I take off my hat. That's obviously a signal?"

"Then they'll see your neat nose and blond hair and know you're not me."

"I believe I'm getting a headache."

"Oh, Peggy, you promised."

"I just bought this blue suit...." Francine allowed a single tear to well in her left eye. Peggy sighed in defeat, but voiced one last protest. "How will I know these guys who follow me are Henry's friends and not some weirdos? I've never met any of Henry's friends. Houston is a different place from San Antonio, and I'm not sure they all aren't rowdy and untrustworthy, coming from a boom town like that." Peggy waved her hands around and thinned her lips.

"There are perfectly nice people in Houston." Francine frowned at her.

"Have you ever seen Henry's naked feet? The whole town is sinking into the Gulf, and they're probably all getting webfooted. You ought to check that out."

"Margaret..."

"Oh, all right." Peggy eyed the purple suit. "The next time you ask me to do something this dumb and I'm stupid enough to agree to it, I've got dibs on picking the outfit. This is..." She couldn't finish but just shuddered.

Francine tsked once in exasperation. "Of all the people I've known all over the world, I've never met your match for dramatics."

"Me? Dramatics?" Peggy puffed with indignation. "I'm not the one who's slipping out of the hotel in disguise!" She ignored the fact that indeed she was. "I'm not the one men follow in droves. I'm not asking *you* to wear that god-awful vile-purple suit with that appallingly yellow hat and lure men away. I'm not—" Peggy rose from the sofa in order to gesture more fully.

"See? That's exactly what I'm talking about. Anyone else would simply change clothes and leave. You're carrying on hysterically over nothing."

"Nothing!" Peggy sputtered.

"Come on. Let's get this over with. Take off your suit." Francine peeled the jacket off Peggy's shoulders. "I hope my suit fits you. You're better built than I."

"I am?" Peggy was surprised.

"You'd have men following you in droves if you just let them. You never allow men the least encouragement. You're probably still a virgin."

"Francine!"

"I think it's because you think every man is after your body, and you're probably right, but you could loosen up a little and have fun in the meantime. Men aren't that wicked. And flirting is marvelous."

"And that's what you're doing to Henry? Another form of flirting?"

"No. I'm sorting things out, Peggy. I really need to know if he likes me and how much he loves me."

"I've read that men like Henry who are very involved in business *avoid* love, because if they really love a woman, they spend too much time and thought on her and neglect their businesses. They think love makes them vulnerable, and they don't want to be that way."

"That's what I have to find out," Francine replied seriously.

"Then this is some sort of test?"

"We'll see." Francine stared soberly at Peggy. "I just want to know what he'll do when he remembers me and checks in with his friends and no one knows where I am."

"This seems childish."

"It's deadly serious."

"Well..." But Peggy didn't finish her sentence. She slid out of her skirt and handed it to Francine; then with great reluctance she picked up the purple skirt from the bed, squinching her eyes to avoid looking at it directly, and put it on. It fit.

Watching her, Francine explained, "I got it a little tight for me."

"You're all heart."

"Once you have it on, *you* won't have to look at it."

The suit was cotton and it was cooler to wear it without a blouse. Peggy put on the jacket and buttoned it. It too fit perfectly. Somehow that didn't thrill her.

"I have a pink scarf that would be—"

"No!"

"I just thought—"

"Never mind."

"We have to switch purses." Francine said as she did just that, then she said, "Try the hat," as she handed it to Peggy and stood watching with alert interest. "Actually, the combination is rather interesting on you, with your blond hair. If you walked with something of a swagger, it would look deliberate and people would find it striking."

"Be quiet." Peggy put on the hat but wouldn't look at it in the mirror.

"It's called flair," Francine went on. "Some people can wear anything and make it look good, and you happen to be one of them."

"You've been very complimentary since I've come in here, Francine, and it makes me nervous. Is there something you're not telling me?"

"Oh, no. I just don't feel competitive with you since I've fallen in love with Henry. I can be honest and tell you you're really smashing."

Peggy gave her "twin" a suspicious, weighing look. "Why do I feel as if your sweet-talk is like a last meal for a doomed woman?"

Francine laughed. Was it forced? Peggy wondered. Then Francine led her to the door and went over her instructions. "Don't be casual when you leave. Be tense, like you're trying to be invisible...."

"In *this* outfit?"

"Sneak out of the elevator and walk around the edge of the lobby as if you're trying to avoid being noticed. Go right on out, get immediately into the car and drive off. Have the tip ready for the car jockey and just leave."

"Francine, I hope this is all worth it."

"Just remember, Peggy, I love you," Francine told her solemnly, as if her friend were going on a voyage of adventure.

Peggy gave her an irritated look, kissed her cheek and left.

One elevator was blocked; the attendant had just finished cleaning it. He smiled nicely at Peggy, indicating that it was free and she could go down in it. Peggy had no clue that it had all been planned that way. She murmured her thanks and donned her colored glasses as she entered the elevator.

Just before the doors closed she was joined by Denims, and they rode down together with her whole system excessively aware of him.

She wondered where he was going, what he did for a living, and if there was some way she could casually look up and see his face. It had again been blocked from her view as he removed his hat to ride with a lady in the elevator.

He had to be old. Young men weren't generally so careful about manners. But his body was exceptional. If he was old, he had kept in good shape. How strange for a man's body to cause hers to react so strongly. A flow of awareness sent little waves washing over her skin, disturbing her. Maybe it was just the excitement of this mad adventure that was making her react so oddly?

In order to try for a peek she took a step away from him in the sinking elevator—but he took a step back. He was trying to get away from her. He must know her body was reacting in a weird way and it embarrassed him.

How could he *possibly* know about her mad response to his being in the same elevator? How could he? If he did know he would probably hit the emergency stop button and get off... escape. He hadn't done that, so he couldn't know.

Peggy was breathing shallowly. It was nerves. He wouldn't
necessarily think it was sexual reaction to his body. It could be
that she was claustrophobic, or that she had asthma. She
opened her mouth and tried to breathe more silently. She was
becoming paranoid. More than likely it was because she was a
virgin.

Virgins could become strange, riding alone in elevators with
men who had devastatingly attractive bodies. What if his face
was ugly? Well, a paper bag over his head would solve that. The
elevator could stop between floors, and they could be trapped
alone there until it could be fixed...hours later. The lights
would be out, and with it dark, it wouldn't matter how he
looked. With that body, it wouldn't matter at all. And they...

The elevator stopped, the door efficiently swished open, and
there was the lobby. They had already come down the whole
four floors. Damn.

Peggy gathered her wits. It was her association with Francine that was addling her brain and causing these crazy illu-
sions. Francine had always influenced her. Peggy took a bracing
breath and stepped into the lobby. Denims had waited courteously until she stepped out—then he followed.

He was following her!

But as soon as he was free of the doors, he turned toward the
desk. He had only followed her through the doors. That was the
only way out of the elevator. She shot a quick look at him, but
he was putting his Stetson back on, and she didn't see anything but a big, strong, brown square hand. A very attractive
hand.

She was probably going mad after all those sedate, logical,
ordinary years—with the only exceptions being the escapades
in which Francine had entangled her. Those episodes were the
only deviations in her orderly life. She was probably flipping
out. How could she think some poor, blameless man had become emotionally entrapped just from riding down four floors
beside her in an elevator?

It must have something to do with being part Indiana Hoosier. Her mother always blamed any weird character traits on

that, and her sudden strange behavior must be Hoosier. She would have to watch it.

How does one sidle around a lobby? It sounded very awkward. She walked briskly around the edge, out the door and there was Francine's car. She put the tip into the outstretched hand of the car jockey and slid into the car, whose engine was idling, waiting for her. She slammed the door, buckled her safety belt, and put the car into gear.

It was a neat car. It tended to run away with her, and she had to curb its eagerness as one would a frisky horse. She eased through traffic, followed the markers and emerged from San Antonio, heading south toward Freer.

This was a silly thing to be doing. She was so involved with how ridiculous it was that she sailed right on past the first truck stop. The car was a love to drive. The day was another gorgeous Texas day, and the car's air-conditioning was coping easily with the August heat.

While she didn't even notice the turnoff for the next truck stop, she did notice that a blue pickup had been behind her for a while. Since there was other traffic it didn't bother her at all. They were supposed to be following her.

How did she know if the blue pickup was following her? Well, for one thing, she always drove just under the speed limit. How many drivers do that? However, the truck had only one man in it, and Francine had said "they," so really it might not be "them," but someone just driving along.

Where was she driving? Good question.

One of the nice things in her life was her independence, which had been assured by her Great Aunt Mattie, her mother's aunt. Mattie had been a spinster who had lived in Temple, about halfway between San Antonio and Dallas. Mattie's family had been in cotton and Old Money. Cotton came before the new dollars from cattle and oil.

How Mattie and Ziggy Mulholland had remained civil long enough to found Matzig, Inc., still baffled Peggy. Ziggy Mulholland had been Great Aunt Mattie's arch enemy, and it was Mattie who had told Peggy, "Men are only out for what they can get." That was what she had told Peggy every time she had come to San Antonio on one of her rare visits.

What Aunt Mattie had done with the rest of her spinster days, Peggy had no clue. And how could she grieve for a woman of eighty-two who had gone to glory in a hot-air balloon race?

Peggy suddenly confronted the fact that Great Aunt Mattie was pure Texas, without a drop of Indiana Hoosier blood, and she had definitely been a little quirky. How interesting.

So because of Aunt Mattie, Peggy had the means to be as independent as she liked. She had no commitments for the rest of August that she couldn't wiggle out of, she had her charge cards for any expenses, and she could buy what clothes she might need easily enough.

Padre Island was really a long, marvelous sandbar protecting the intercoastal traffic along the Texas shores. Peggy could go there and bury that purple suit in the sand somewhere and rid the world of such a shocking thing. Along with the ugly yellow hat.

There went another truck stop. She would have to settle down and pay attention. But...if Francine wanted to get away from her followers, why not give her more time?

What if they weren't fooled and hadn't followed her? She slowed down to see if the blue pickup would slow down or if it would pass her. It went on by. Well, that shot that theory down. He hadn't been following her.

She watched to see if anyone else who came along looked at her or dawdled behind her. No one did. They had never been following her at all! Great. The whole stupid thing was a complete failure. She might just as well go on back.

But then, she was this far along, so why *not* go on over to the coast? When she came to a highway phone, she stopped, phoned home, and told the housekeeper, "I think I'll go on over to the coast for a couple of days. Would you call Francine and tell her she'll get her car back when I get back?"

"Are you being held for ransom?" the housekeeper demanded.

"No." Perhaps being dramatic was a Texas trait? "I'm just helping Francine out. I have her car and it's a long story. I'll let you know where I am, but it could be a day or two. 'Bye."

"Kids these days...." The housekeeper was still being quarrelsome when Peggy said goodbye a second time and eased the phone onto the hook.

So. She was free. Just then the blue pickup came back along down the highway, and the man inside looked at her from under a shadowy Stetson. It was a level look that went through her in a puzzling way.

There had been no reason for him to come back...unless... Maybe the game was still on? Maybe she *had* lured Francine's watchdogs off on this false trail? Maybe.

Well, she was certainly far enough away that Francine would have had time enough for any sort of deception she wanted. Peggy could now "unmask" by finding a truck stop and removing her hat, thereby betraying the fact that she was not Francine and that the watchdogs had been fooled.

How would they take that? In her experience men did not much like being fooled. When the followers saw that they had been deliberately misled, what would they do? That is, what would *he* do? He was alone in the blue pickup. He would know the instant she took off that hat that he had been tricked. Who in the world would wear that purple suit with that hat if not for a disguise? He would know.

Well. "The time has come, the Walrus said..." She got back into Francine's car and went on south. It wasn't long before she caught a glimpse of the blue pickup hanging farther back, being very discreet about following her. It was one of the watchdogs, all right. And he thought she was Francine. Peggy smiled as she looked for a truck stop.

What she found was a roadblock. She slowed cautiously. Bales of hay were stacked on her side of the highway in front of a green pickup truck, and three men were directing traffic. There was no traffic. Just her...and the blue pickup behind her.

The roadblockers were all cheerful, smiling, well dressed in casual ranch clothes, healthy and young. Henry's friends? White slavers? Maniacal ax murderers? What had Francine gotten her into?

She rolled to a stop, her doors locked, and as one of the men approached courteously, she opened her window only a sliver and waited.

"A pig transport turned over down the road, honey, and it's a mess. Best turn off and go thataway. It's only for a mile, to detour around, and then you take the first turn back to the highway."

She eyed the two narrow wheel ruts going down off the road into the short lacy mesquite trees, and she felt a qualm. "Where's the highway patrol?"

He replied easily, "We're just helping out till they git here. This way we don't have to help round up all them hysterical messy pigs."

From behind her dark glasses she considered him. He appeared to be telling the truth. His words were logical.

Just then the blue pickup pulled up behind her and another of the three roadblockers called out with cheerful humor that the pig transport had turned over.

In her rearview mirror she could see the man in the pickup touch his hat brim, back his truck, pull around her along the shoulder of the highway and head off down the detour.

He wasn't following her. If he had been, he would have waited to see what she was going to do. She might turn around and go back the other way for all he knew, but instead of waiting for her to decide, he had just gone off like that.

Peggy debated. Her roadblocker stood there admiring Francine's car and patiently waiting as he glanced up and down the highway. He was very relaxed and easy. He didn't urge her along. He had simply explained the situation. Now it was up to her to do...whatever she wanted.

She did not particularly want to go back to town. She looked at the rutted lane that headed under the mesquite tress, and it looked cool and different. She studied the three men. They were unhurried, talking softly with an occasional grin, seeming to ignore her, but aiming enough glances her way to show they were interested in a pretty girl.

Pretty? In that suit and hat? They weren't interested—they were *wary*. For all they knew she might explode out of that red car in that purple suit and ghastly yellow hat and attack them! They were out there all alone, too, and they had no idea what she might do to them.

There was still no traffic as far down the road in back of her as she could see. She would be alone in that shady lane. It looked dry, no bogs, no quicksand. She would do it.

As she turned her wheel the man beside her car brought his attention back to her and smiled politely. She nodded once in courteous response and slowly left the highway.

It was a charming lane, shaded from the hot August sun. A fox crossed ahead of her and paused, watching, before it vanished. How amazing. There were occasional oaks, and some hackberry trees mixed with the mesquite and cactus. The lane didn't seem to turn back toward the highway but just continued on west.

How far had she come? The road had become quite sandy, and up ahead through the trees there was a tiny stream. How lovely! She followed the road around a bend and there, blocking the track, was the blue pickup!

Her car coasted to a stop as she thought, so that's how he looks, and she realized he was Denims from the elevator. His face matched his gorgeous body—and he was one of Henry's friends. He *had* been following her, and there she was—and there he was.

Two

———

He was leaning against the side of his blue pickup truck, and he had one strong leg bent so his booted foot rested on the step. He was magnificent. He lifted one hand up to nudge back his Stetson, and his grin was white in his tanned face. He was rugged and masculine. Mind-boggling. She gaped.

He indicated the narrow, clear, shallow stream with one casual hand. Her eyes followed his motion and she looked at it. The track appeared to cross the tiny creek. She looked back to him, her eyes drawn like filings to a magnet, as he called in a thrillingly deep voice, "Quicksand," and grinned.

Was he teasing her? If she looked carefully, she could see that the real track actually did not cross but curved alongside the stream; however, his pickup blocked it. There was no way to get past him to follow the original track, and there wasn't room to turn around. If she wanted to leave without confronting him, she would have to back up all the way to the highway. Or she could cross the stream.

She studied him as he stood there, and it was a pleasure. She became aware that he was very amused, waiting to see what she would do. He obviously thought he had her in a trap. Not her, of course, but Francine. He thought he had won. Well, she would fool *him*. All she had to do was step from her car, take off that ghastly yellow hat and her sunglasses, and show him she was not Francine. That was all she had to do.

But he slouched there so beautifully confident, and his slight smile was so masculinely smug, that she lifted her foot from the brake, gave him a slight, superior smile, and drove gently into the stream.

He watched her with indulgent interest, but he didn't move.

She felt her front wheels sink into the sand as they moved into the stream, and she gave the car a little gas to encourage it, but the front wheels continued to sink very slowly. There *was* quicksand, and her front wheels were in it.

By the time he came to the driver's door, the water was up to her front hubcaps. His deep voice repeated reasonably, "Quicksand." And he did try not to smile.

Disgusted, she figured she had better get out before the whole car was swallowed up, leaving her to be dug up in a million years, when the mutants would be astounded by the sporty car and the odd bones of a humanoid lying in the tatters of the awful purple suit and the yellow hat. She unlocked the door, and he opened it courteously as he offered a hand to help her out. She did remember to take the keys and her purse.

Peggy stood beside him, extremely conscious of him, and they watched the front of Francine's car as it settled just a little more. Now what could she say? He had warned her...with a big, cheerful grin. Had he known that if he had been serious then she wouldn't have tried it? But she hadn't been able to resist driving across the stream to escape for a little longer before she revealed she was not Francine.

This was as good a time as any. She removed her sunglasses with some flair, and then she grasped the front of the hat, skimmed it off, then turned to give him a faintly superior, supercilious smile of triumph.

His expression did not change. He studied her face with pleasure, and his faint smile crinkled the lines around his eyes, lines that had been etched in his young face by laughter and squinting into the strong Texas sunlight. He was not yet thirty. He had probably been out in the boondocks to escape the women for a while so he could rest up.

"Hullo, Francine," he said with quiet humor.

That did startle her. "I'm not Francine."

"Good try." His head gave a slow, slight bow of acknowledgment. His blue eyes were filled with laughter. His eyelashes were tipped white from the sun, almost camouflaging their length. His left front tooth had a fascinating chip out of it.

"Who are you?" she asked, haughtily in control.

"Name's Joe." His body was relaxed and he appeared unthreatening as they stood there in the silence. Peggy became aware of the sound of an approaching truck.

She frowned. He shifted and moved to stand between her and the approaching vehicle. It was easily done; he was marvelously coordinated. He also kept one eye on her. Did he think she would bolt?

Obviously this Joe person knew Henry. Why didn't he know she was not Francine? Who was coming? And after thinking who it could be, she was not at all surprised to see the green pickup from the highway roadblock. She put her hands on her hips and assumed a belligerent stance.

The green pickup stopped in a cloud of sandy dust, and the three men boisterously slammed out of the truck. With a decided lack of tact they laughed over the blocked road and her sinking car. They didn't crowd her. Two stayed back lounging against the front of their truck, and the one who had talked to her on the highway came several steps forward, but Joe was still between them and her.

Joe immediately called to them, "She claims she's not Francine, but we know she is. She's still trying to fool us."

That made the three hesitate, and they looked at Joe, then beyond him at Peggy, then back to Joe, whose face she could not see.

"That right?" Roadblocker One finally asked cautiously, noncommittal.

"That is correct," she put in firmly. "I am Margaret Indiana Dillon."

"Indiana?" Roadblocker Two asked Number Three politely.

"Foreign blood," Three replied. "Probably a half-breed. Indiana-Texan. They're a tricky bunch."

"I am not Francine!"

"You look like her," Roadblocker Two remarked.

"I do not either!"

"Oh. Hostile." Two raised his eyebrows to the other roadblockers. Then they ignored her and spoke among themselves. "What are we supposed to do about her now we have her?"

"I'll take care of her," Joe told them.

"Didn't you tell her about the quicksand?" Roadblocker One asked.

"Sure," Joe replied.

"It seemed to me there were tracks on the other side." Peggy was stridently defensive.

"Well, there *are*!" was the reply. "But that's from trucks being dragged out on the other side with mules."

"Then—" Peggy turned to look at Francine's car "—you mean the car won't sink out of sight?"

"Naw. It's only a little bit. There's a rock shelf just under there. But getting it out'll be fun. Quicksand's reluctant to give up anything."

"With both your trucks, couldn't you do that now?"

"Well..." Roadblocker One began.

"No," interrupted Joe. "We don't have any rope."

Peggy was sure that surprised the roadblockers, and that they did have ropes, but they all agreed with Joe. "Naw, don't have any rope," said Two, and the rest agreed, shaking their heads.

She watched them suspiciously. Their twangs and incomplete sentences seemed to be drawn out and deliberate. "Do you know Francine?" she demanded of the three.

"Just met her." "Standing right there." "Pretty girl." They grinned at her, while Joe turned lazily to watch her.

"But you do know the man Francine is dating?"

Joe smiled at her and told the three, "Tell Francine his name."

Again the three men glanced oddly at Joe before Number Three volunteered, "Henry Patterson."

"Then you do know Henry?"

"Yep." "Sure do." "Why?" Their replies came all at once.

"But you've never met Francine?"

Again they hesitated and their eyes slid to Joe. Then One replied, "We're with Joe," whatever that could mean.

"Henry gave Francine his signet ring. Look. No ring." Peggy showed them her bare hands.

Joe scolded, "Now, Francine, what have you gone and done with your ring?"

And Roadblocker Two chimed in with, "Did you hock it before you ran away?"

"I am not running away...."

"Hah!" Joe laughed. "She said 'I.' She's just admitted she's Francine and pretending she isn't running away from good old Henry."

Peggy put both her hands in her hair and shrieked.

"Man, she can do that real good." "Women tend to." "Touchy, isn't she?" The roadblockers' faces were pleasantly patient.

Agitated, she walked around in a circle, her heels sinking in the sand, as the four relaxed men watched her. Her fists were clenched, as were her teeth, and her breath was harsh with temper. "My *driver's* license! Ah-*hah*!" She zipped open her purse and began to dig into it.

Roadblocker One observed to Number Three, "Woman drives into quicksand, and she has a driver's license! Things are sure getting lax." He shook his head in slow disapproval.

Three replied soothingly, "Women are precious. We have to let them think they know what they're doing. They're such pretty, soft little things."

"True. But giving a woman a license when she'll drive through quicksand seems rash."

"See?" Peggy triumphantly held up her wallet. "Look! Margaret Indiana Dillon." She lifted her chin and pointed to the typically ghastly picture perpetrated by license bureaux everywhere. "That's me!" And she put her thumb to her nice chest.

"I," One corrected.

How strange for such a grammatically loose speaker to correct her. That had attracted a corner of her mind and she frowned.

But Joe said, "That's smart, Francine. What about that purple suit that Francine wore into the hotel? Henry pointed you out to me once, you know. And you're driving Francine's car. That's her license plate. Where did you get Margaret Indiana Dillon's driver's license? Did you mug some poor unsuspecting girl?"

Why should the sound of her name on his lips said in his marvelous voice paralyze her brain? Turn her knees weak? Cross her eyes?

While she was figuring that out, Roadblocker Three asked, "What you going to do about her, Joe?"

"Yeah." Number Two also wanted an answer.

"I'll take her over to the cabin."

"Now, Joe," cautioned One, who had spoken to Peggy on the highway.

But Joe interrupted quickly. "I know what I'm doing! Trust me. Tell Henry where I am."

Suddenly Peggy flipped off her fragile high heels and, stocking-footed, she fled past them all, running back down the track.

"Whoops!" One yelled. "There she goes!"

"I got her. I got her," called Joe as if she were a fly ball. He let her run deliberately to allow her to think she had a chance, but then he ran circles around her. How rude of him to show off that way! He caught her so easily. And he held her, and he hugged her to him, and he laughed deep in his chest.

"Easy now, easy," he said as the others caught up to them. His breathing was normal, but hers was rasping, and she fought tears of frustration.

"You're okay," Roadblocker One assured her seriously.

"Nobody's going to hurt you," promised Joe. "I swear that on my honor." And with the last sentence he looked up at the three other men as they watched his face. Then they nodded or slowly relaxed as if they had been reassured. Now that was odd. Why should he reassure *them*? Joe kept an arm around her as he turned her back toward the trucks.

"You're all right," Three told Peggy. "Don't fret."

"Around here," Roadblocker One lectured her, "you gotta be careful about quicksand and snakes. Don't you ever go off the track. It's not safe."

Roadblocker Two turned to Joe and added, "We'd better leave Faraday with you in case she tries to get away again." He frowned at Peggy. "You could get lost out here real easy. This is serious. Pay attention."

"Faraday?"

"Henry's dog." He gestured to the back of the green pickup, where a huge, short-legged, floppy-eared ugly dog dozed indifferently. She was terrified of dogs and drew back sharply.

"Don't be afraid," Roadblocker One soothed her. "We're all friends of Henry's, and we know how careful Joe will be of you...Francine."

"I am not Francine," Peggy declared yet again.

"Faraday won't actually eat you," One contributed. "He's just the best tracking dog there is—when he's in the mood."

"He's ugly, and I hate dogs."

"Shhhhh," Joe scolded her. "How can you say something like that right in front of him that way? Shame on you." He clicked his tongue in censure, and the others enjoyed that.

"Do you have a CB radio in your truck?" Peggy demanded.

After a glance at Joe the rest shook their heads solemnly.

"Then take me to a phone. I'll call Henry and *prove* I'm not Francine."

"Honey, he's out in the field and won't be back for...a while." The three roadblockers turned their eyes to Joe, and he said, "It's okay." Palm down, he spread the fingers of one hand in a calming gesture.

"I don't much like this," Roadblocker One said. "I think one of us ought to stay with you."

"No need. You all have things to do, and Henry will appreciate how you've helped."

"You're sure she's..." the second roadblocker began.

"No problem." Joe was firm. "You all can take off. I'll handle it from here on."

The men managed to rouse Faraday and get him down from the green pickup and into the blue one, and the dog sat in the middle of the seat in the cab, his face, ears, and skin all drooping.

It was then that Peggy made her move. Since it was obvious that the three roadblockers had some reservations about leaving her alone with Joe, she walked over to the green pickup and got in.

Joe followed right along after her and pulled her back out. She swung her fist and missed him entirely. He gathered her close against him, shushing her like a baby or a puppy or something helpless. She was *not* helpless—if he would just let go—and it made her mad that he didn't.

Red-faced from her struggles, she shouted, "Help me!" to the three frozen witnesses. Since there were three of them to one of Joe, they should be able to handle him, although he was very quick and strong.

"Joe..." began One.

"Never mind." Joe wasn't even panting. "It'll be okay. I promise."

"You're sure, Rickity?" asked Two.

"Trust me," Joe replied mildly. Then, more firmly, he directed, "Go *on*, now. With you all gone, she'll settle down."

She kicked him in the shin, but she was too close to him and stocking-footed, so it wasn't very effective. He only hushed her again, holding her tightly, and his chest rumbled as if he were purring. His eyes were bright, and the crinkles at their corners showed he was amused. He was enjoying holding her.

How shocking! He was enjoying it. He thought she was Francine and that she was Henry's woman, and he was hugging her tightly with her squashed up against his hard body...and he was enjoying it. Shame on him!

She wiggled and squirmed, and his purr sounded in her ear and through her chest, and she didn't even notice when the green pickup drove off.

She finally quit struggling, and they stood there plastered to each other. There was a light breeze, and she heard the whisper of the leaves moving; the water was hushed, and there were birds. After the roar of the green truck faded gradually away, there was a great deal of silence.

She moved her chin up and looked into his blue eyes with the white tipped lashes and dark brows. "Did they back all the way to the highway, or did they turn around?"

His crinkles deepened, and he managed to tighten his arm as he replied, "I didn't notice."

"Let go."

"In a minute."

"Now."

"Do I have to?"

"Yes."

"Well—for now." He reluctantly loosened his arms, taking his own sweet time, but he didn't move. She had to brace herself with her hands on his chest in order to step away from him. And it shocked her that she really wanted to be back against him. She wished she were wearing anything but that damned purple suit. Ugh. She would look better naked...and the image of her naked with him made her blush.

She lifted her chin. The best defense was a good offense. "If you're holding me for ransom," she said firmly and rather primly, "there's no one to pay it." She looked up into his eyes, then down, as she lied, "I'm an orphan."

"Aw. I've never heard such a sad story in all my life."

Her eyes darted back to his, but his face was pleasantly sober and apparently serious. She tried another tack. "Henry will clobber you."

"Henry isn't for you," Joe told her. "Believe me."

"I am not Francine."

"Good. Then Henry will have no reason to clobber me, will he? We'll just stay at the cabin until he turns up."

"I'm not getting into that truck with that dog."

"Faraday doesn't realize he's a dog, and he's very sensitive. You have to watch what you say around him, or he'll go into a decline."

"I'll walk." She took a firm, stocking-footed step away, but he reached out and clamped his fingers on her arm.

He resettled his hat low on his forehead, then let go of her. "Don't be contrary. Nobody loves a contrary woman."

She stretched her mouth in a nasty smile over her clenched teeth and enunciated, "Then, let's do it my way. Pull my car out and I'll go home."

"And miss this great adventure? Nonsense, woman. Come along nice like, and let's get to the cabin." As he reached for her arm she lifted it up out of his reach, and his fingers closed on air. "Honey, don't rile me. I've just quit smoking and my temper isn't the best." He reached for her again, but she simply sat down on the track.

Effortlessly he leaned over, picked her up, put her over his shoulder and carried her to the truck. He held her with one hand on her rump and the other locked around her knees, and he told Faraday in a very insensitive way, "Over in back, dog, hustle up."

After an indignant look, the dog heaved himself up and, with audible grunts of effort, carefully made it over into the back of the truck bed. Amazing.

Joe leaned forward as he eased Peggy onto the front seat; then he closed the door and held the sill with both hands as he looked at her. His smile began, the crinkles deepening; he was obviously pleased about the situation.

She said aloofly, "My shoes."

He lifted his hand to resettle his hat again as he replied, "Ah, yes. Shoes. Hold still."

He went around the truck and picked up her discarded shoes as she put her hand on the door handle for one more try at escape, but she found his eyes quickly on her as if he had read her mind, so she just sat there. Her shoes looked small and fragile in his hands, and he patted them together to shake some of the sand from them. Then he got into the truck and handed them to her. She put them on, but she left the yellow hat back in the sinking car.

She gave Francine's car a quick look. Actually it didn't appear to have gone down any more than it had earlier. She watched while he backed the truck and turned, and she happened to look over into the truck bed, where she saw the dog flopped with a long-suffering look on a loose coil of rope. Rope!

"You have a rope in the back."

His look of surprise was exaggerated. "Well, I do declare that's so."

"You knew it."

"Honey, I didn't get you into that quicksand to get you out again. That wasn't a part of the plan."

"You deliberately tricked me into driving into the quicksand?"

"Naturally."

She sputtered, and he chuckled as he drove easily, the breeze ruffling his shirt sleeve where his arm rested along the windowsill. Eventually they drove out of the mesquite trees and into a cleared area where there had once been an orange grove.

The trees had frozen a time or two, and they hadn't been replanted or cared for. Trash trees and bushes were taking over. Weeds grew along the way and tipped over onto the track, making it even narrower.

"You wouldn't want to walk on this track along here," Joe told her. "With the weeds so thick all the snakes use the track because it makes it easier for them to move along." He gave her a quick, measuring glance.

She looked at him in horror, but by then he was looking forward and his face was sober and bland, as if he were discussing the weather—which was as beautiful as usual.

She looked along the track in front of them, then out across the bent and broken trees. A few had survived and were heavy with fruit. Some trees had only partially died, and those, too, had fruit.

"Do the oranges just go to waste?"

"No. There are some families around about that—" he shot a look at her, then he continued firmly "—that live a long way off. Henry gives them the oranges. They have big families. There isn't enough fruit to gather commercially, but it's a windfall for them. Even though they do live quite a way from here."

Why was he stressing how far away they lived? So she wouldn't try to find them?

He went on, "There are gila monsters around here, too, besides the rattlesnakes. And wolves."

"No wolves." She was sure of that.

"Only recently they've sighted some wolves."

"There has never been an authenticated case of wolves attacking people. Dog packs do, but—"

"And dog packs," he added earnestly. "It's a dangerous place."

"Then let's get my car out of the sand and we'll go back to the safe city."

He resettled his hat on his head, looked briefly out his window and replied, "Nope. I have to wait at the cabin for Henry." He slid a look over at her as he added, "With you."

That caused a quake in her lower body and stopped her breathing entirely. She had to cough to get her respiratory system started again; it was like kicking a furnace. The ploy almost failed to work when she foolishly glanced back at him. After that she just looked out her window and was silent, but breathing.

With all Henry's money, Peggy realized what the "cabin" would be like. There would be a guest closet with spare clothes of various sizes, and she could get rid of the ghastly purple rag she was wearing.

The first thing she would do would be to swim. She just hoped the pool wasn't heated. A soak in the Jacuzzi, a refreshingly cool swim, and then she would lie in a hammock in the shade on the terrace. Anyone as civilized as Henry would have a shaded terrace facing the Gulf breezes. The constant southeast Gulf breeze made most of Texas pleasant all summer.

She was hungry and wondered what would be served for dinner. This close to the Gulf it could well be shrimp. In all probability she would survive her "captivity" very easily. She smiled and allowed herself a quick peek at Joe. She might as well be civil.

"Did I hear one of the roadblockers call you Rick? Or Rickity? It sounded more like Rickity."

He nodded. "My...second name's Richards. But I was nicknamed Rickity at one time. In my foolish youth, a couple of years back, I had to learn the hard way that there are things that just don't give in to determination. I limped a lot in those days, and wore slings and eye patches. I have learned—with my greater maturity—that there are some things I need to walk around."

In a perfectly pleasant tone she said, "You let me go, or you'll be limping again."

He grinned, his eyes crinkling. "I find it very difficult to walk around you."

A flood of excitement went up her back into her scalp. It was a good thing the breeze was streaming through the cab so when her hair stood up from the electrical reaction to him, it appeared to be from a capricious gust of wind.

She desperately sought distracting conversation. "How much farther is it?"

"A ways."

"How far have we come?"

He grinned and gave her a very sensual look. "Not nearly far enough."

"If Henry has hired you to seduce Francine, I am *not* Francine and you are wasting all that charm."

"Do you find me charming?"

"You know *exactly* what I mean," she scolded like a prude. And he laughed.

Tartly she retorted, "If you went a little faster, we would get there quicker."

"And jostle Faraday?" Joe's face registered supreme shock. "Henry would never forgive me! Neither would Faraday."

She turned and looked back at the dog, who rolled a stoic eye at her. "How could anyone care about that ugly dog?"

"Shhhh. Not so loud."

She sighed with impatience. "The first thing I'm going to do is swim."

"It might be just a tad cool," he cautioned.

"Good. I'm so mad, the water will steam when I dive in."

"If I'd known water would calm you, I'd have rolled you in the creek, it being too shallow for a swim," he hastily explained.

"And I would have sunk with the car."

"No, no. I know where the quicksand lies. I'd be very, very careful not to lose you."

Those last words sent another foolish wave of electric excitement up her back. "Henry must have a strong hold on you—for you to do this silly errand for him."

"Henry and I understand each other."

"Have you known each other long?"

"A long time."

"Then why don't you know I'm *not* Francine?"

"Honey, you're wearing a purple suit and you're driving a red car. How many women wearing purple suits drive red cars?"

"Well, yes. But you see, Francine wanted Henry to come look for her and—"

"He'll be here as soon as he gets free. Just be patient."

"*I'm not Francine; I'm Margaret Indiana Dillon!*"

"We'll be there soon, and then you can have that nice, calming swim. I guarantee it'll cool you off."

"Men!" she seethed, her bosom heaving.

"You like men?" he asked with cheerful interest.

"They are the most baffling species women have to contend with!" Her hands were back in her hair.

"We're almost there," he said comfortingly. "The road washes out with the rains—"

"What rains?"

"Now, now. Don't start on our beautiful Texas weather. When the liquid sunshine falls over this fair state, it sometimes happens that it washes over this part of the road and rearranges it so it's just a little bit uneven. Now, you wouldn't want Faraday to be uncomfortable, would you?"

"Faraday should walk. He's too fat."

"That's muscle."

That made her laugh.

He tilted back his Stetson and grinned at her. "My, that's a pretty sound." Since he was going so slow, he could look at her. "You pleasure my eyes." His voice was husky.

"If you think I'm Francine, how can you explain flirting with me?" She tilted her head, trying to pretend she didn't like what he was doing.

"Flirting?" He appeared surprised. "I thought I was just appreciating." He frowned as he considered the idea seriously, then he admitted, "There might have been a tiny bit of flirt creeping in there. I'll watch it."

That dismayed her, and she was silent, biting her errant tongue. They crept along in silence. Faraday grunted over the shifting of his flab, and Joe called encouragement to the dog.

"There's the windmill!" Joe pointed. "That means we're almost there." Faraday barked. He must have spotted the windmill, too.

"Where's the cabin?" Peggy asked.

"Just over that rise. We'll make it yet! Then you can swim."

"Does...Faraday swim, too?" she asked suspiciously.

"I don't think you could get him to," Joe said regretfully. "He's a watcher."

"I wouldn't *want* him in the pool."

"Don't you like dogs?"

"Not at all."

"How astonishing. A warped childhood?"

"Have you taken a close look at that dog? He looks as if he was put together by a committee that only communicated by phone."

That made Joe laugh.

The truck inched up the tortured lane to the top of the rise, but the cabin still wasn't in sight. Peggy looked around. It was a lovely view. How strange that this hill hadn't been used as the location of the cabin.

Over yonder was a small river that curved along the bottom of a bluff; the meadow below was dotted with mesquite, and in the spring, it was probably a blanket of wildflowers: bluebonnets, fire wheels, Indian paintbrushes, buttercups, verbena.

The nearby windmill rode the breeze and could be adjusted to pump water into the pond at its feet. To one side was a rotten shack with weeds growing high and junk scattered in the yard. It was rather picturesque, with its weather-beaten boards and tin roof, sitting back under the shade of a large oak.

"Where's the cabin?" she asked as they eased toward the shack.

"Right there."

"Where?" She turned her head, sure she was missing something.

"There in front of you." He pointed straight ahead.

All she could see was the…"You mean…? The…shack?"

"Yeah." He looked at her to see what the problem was.

"That shack, right there, is Henry's…*cabin*?"

He looked at it, then back at her, and replied, "Sure," as if to ask, what could be more obvious? "There," he said with satisfaction as they rolled to a stop. He opened his door and stepped out. "I'll help you out."

She hadn't moved. She couldn't believe it. That shack? That was Henry's *cabin*? Joe was teasing. After he had enjoyed his little joke, he would take her to the real cabin.

Joe was getting Faraday out of the back of the truck. She had thought he'd meant he would help her, but he had been talking to the dog.

She was setting one high heel down to the ground when he reached her side, and he smiled at her as he resettled his Stetson and said, "Now you can swim in the pool and cool off."

"What pool?" She looked around for a nonexistent swimming pool.

"Over there by the windmill."

"The farm pond?" She was incredulous. "With *mud*?"

"Sure."

Even then she was not convinced. What finally convinced her was that she saw that the track ended there at the shack. It didn't go anywhere else. They had arrived at their destination, and the shack was it.

Three

When they crossed the sagging porch Peggy found it was not just a shack, it was a one-room shack. The inside of the building was unfinished and the studding was exposed. The room had the door to the porch on one side, and a tall, very narrow window on each of the other three sides. She could have stood in the middle of the room and swung a broom and touched all four walls.

The reason she couldn't swing that broom was because crammed inside there were a big rumpled bed, a refrigerator, a freezer and two cupboards. How astonishing. There was also a table with two chairs, and a single light bulb hanging from the middle of the ceiling, and none of it was tidy.

The bed had an elaborately curlicued iron bedstead with scaling paint, and it took up almost a fourth of the cabin. There was another "window" up near the ceiling that was really a ragged, splintered hole which had screening tacked over it.

"What happened up there?"

"Shotgun went off."

"Oh." Under the circumstances, she hesitated to ask why it had gone off just over the bed that way.

Since there was a plank ceiling, and the tin roof was above that with an air space between, it was relatively cool in the shack under that big oak tree. She looked at the dirty, dusty bedding and the dirty, dusty chairs and she didn't want to set even that purple suit down anywhere.

Quite obviously there would be no guest closet, and until she left here, that ghastly purple suit was all she would have to wear.

She looked over at Joe, who was leaning against the door-jamb, and she said in a perfectly controlled voice, "Okay. The joke's over. Take me back to my car and pull it out. You have a rope."

"You're a terrible houseguest," he chided. "That was purely rude."

"I want to go home," she went on very seriously. "I am not Francine, and I see no reason to endure being in this shack until you are convinced of that. Look at my driver's license. My picture is on it." She enunciated her words as if she were speaking to an idiot. "I am blond. Francine is a brunette."

"We'll wait a while and watch the hair roots."

She flung her purse at him and tried to reach the door as he dodged the purse, but he stretched out a strong arm and effortlessly stopped her. Her eyes flashed, she breathed hard, and she was really mad.

"It won't be for long," he coaxed her. "Just a day or two."

"A day or *two*?" she huffed. "You *are* crazy!"

"Actually I've never been more sane. Bide with me and relax, honey. No harm will come to you, I promise."

"And you'll sleep in the truck," she commanded.

"Of course! Unless you want me here beside you...on the floor, of course...so that you won't worry about the rattlers or the gila monsters or the wo...dog packs."

She gave him a killing look; then she again surveyed the bed. She looked up at him, and he returned her gaze. He smiled just a little at her, and his eyes were very kind. "Don't be scared," he told her in a soft rumble.

"Take me home."

"Not yet, honey. I will, but not for a while." And one of his hands smoothed the back of her silky head.

They stood there together in the silence, and Faraday woofed at the door.

She jerked up and declared, "That dog does *not* come in this house—shack!"

Joe agreed. "It's too dirty for him."

She shoved herself away from Joe, put her fists on her hips and glared at the interior of the shack. Behind the refrigerator there was a broom whose bristles looked as if they had permanently given in to a strong wind. There were also a bucket, a mop and a pan.

While she looked around, he opened the freezer and gave her a lime Popsicle, then took Faraday two ice cream bars. He had a beer.

Relishing the Popsicle, she went outside. There was a pump in the yard, and she found a tub hanging from a nail on the windmill side of the shack. At the back corner of each side of the shack was a wooden rain barrel, almost full, and swimming inside were goldfish!

Joe was trailing along behind her and he explained, "They eat the mosquito eggs."

"You're going to help."

"Eat mosquito eggs?" He appeared surprised.

She was patient. "Clean this place."

"Why? What's wrong with it?" He looked around. "You want me to mow the weeds? There isn't any mower."

"Now, we're going to scrub out the shack."

"Good Lord."

"First we'll strip that bed and throw the sheets and blankets into the pond."

"You'll kill the fish!"

She thinned her lips and glared at him.

He said, "There's a big barrel at the bottom of the windmill. It's full of sun-warmed water. After your bath, you can soak the sheets and anything else and then hang them on the mill braces."

"Get the rope from the back of the truck and string it from the oak to the mill."

"The mill braces are already there. Why not use them?"

"There are dirty clothes on the bed and in that basket."

"Someone else can wash them. I didn't bring you here to clean and wash clothes."

"Why *did* you bring me here?"

He smiled at her, genuinely amused, and then chose his words with care. "To wait for Henry."

"If it comes to pass that I have to sleep in that bed, it's going to be clean." She stomped back inside the shack and he followed.

"What a picky woman you are." He shook his head in wonder.

"And there's the chance that something in that bunch of clothes will fit me, and I can get out of this hot, long-sleeved, god-awful suit."

"I like purple on you."

"We've already proven you're crazy, so your opinion doesn't carry much weight."

He took off his shirt and hung it on a wall peg, then put his hat on the same peg. His hair was thick and brown and perfectly straight. He had a beautiful torso, strong and brown. His muscles rolled under his skin, and she sneaked peeks his way.

He encouraged her to get comfortable, too, and offered to hang up her suit coat, but it was all she had to wear and she declined. She did rip out the sleeves of the jacket. She hated that suit and took pleasure in the act. She would never in this world *ever* wear purple again. Then she took off her shoes and set them in Joe's truck, where they would be safe.

The privy was surprisingly sturdy and scrupulously clean. It, too, was dusty, but Joe scrubbed it out first. He did all the heavy work, and they worked well together.

He managed to relieve her of almost everything she started, yet he kept her busy enough with little things that she appeared occupied and wasn't aware how he had maneuvered her.

They wrestled the mattress outside to beat it and prop it against some of the remaining cedar fence posts in the sun to air; then they carried the dirty clothes and bedding out to the windmill. Joe carried the tin tub and put it on a wash bench on the concrete slab under the mill structure.

He scooped warm water into the tub, over the soap beads which could be used in any temperature water, and he put a scrub board into the tub and scrubbed everything as if he had done it before. How interesting.

She rinsed the clothes; he wrung them, his muscles bulging, and hung them over the line. And after the bed linens and blankets were draped over the mill braces and held in place with rocks, they attacked the shack.

It didn't take long until it was swept and then scrubbed. He willingly carried buckets of water and said she was drowning the termites.

"Termites?" she asked, horrible mental pictures racing through her brain.

"With no air space between the floor and the ground, there are bound to be termites."

"Do they bite?"

"Only wood."

Eventually they stood and viewed the results of their labor. It didn't look better, only cleaner. "It needs paint," she judged.

He laughed. "I thought that would be the next thing to occur to you. Forget it." He grinned at her. "Now we can swim."

Everything in the house was drying. There was nothing that could be used as a bathing suit. She eyed him, then said, "Let's go."

He whooped in delight and hustled her back past the drying clothes to the windmill's pond. She looked at the muddy bank and hesitated. But he went over and retrieved the wooden wash bench and pressed it into the mud at the side of the pond so that it was a step down and an unmuddy launch for a dive. Then he stood back and undid his trousers.

Still clothed, she immediately turned, stepped down onto the bench and dived into the water—purple suit, pantyhose, and all. She surfaced and blew a shocked breath. It was frigidly cold.

How could it be that cold? It was probably very deep. She peeked back at Joe as he hit the water. She saw his trousers lying over the water pipe which supplied water to the pond. Was he naked?

He surfaced next to her and laughed at her. "Washing your suit? It'll probably shrink, and you'll be a scandal."

"There are jeans and shirts on the line," she replied in a prissy way. "I told you I could use those."

"So that's why you got so domestic! I thought you were just a very tidy girl."

"I'm a woman."

"Oh, yes." He closed his eyes and sank down into the water.

Faraday had taken his time coming to the pond, and he walked as if he wore shoes that were too tight. There was never any threat of his joining them. He simply watched the strange behavior of the man and woman in the pond. Interesting.

They had to swim to stay warm, and they did for a while, but he wouldn't be serious, and he teased and played. She had a terrible time remembering she was mad, and that she didn't want to be there.

When she swam to the bench to leave the pond, he beat her there, lifted himself effortlessly to the bench—he was wearing red briefs—then reached and lifted her from the water as if she were constructed of thistledown.

Her suit hadn't shrunk, but it was running with water and draggy. He took an almost-dry sheet from the brace, held it up, and closed his eyes as he grinned and said, "I won't watch if you want to strip, and then you can become a Roman in this sheet."

She hesitated. Each time she looked at him he did seem to have his eyes closed, but with his lashes, she could not be ab-

solutely sure. So she turned her back and quickly rid herself of
the god-awful purple suit.

She took hold of the top of the sheet, but he didn't let go. His
eyes opened, and he looked at her quickly. She crowded close
to the sheet—and him—so that he could not see her body. He
smiled and explained, "Oh, I thought you were just peeking
over the top." Then he finally released the sheet.

Her tongue couldn't sort one thing to say from the rush of
scolding that flooded her mind, so she was back to sputtering.
Also, she had never draped herself in a sheet before, and fumbled around with it until he said, "No, no, no, no." Leaving her
one end, he folded the other and adjusted the rest of the sheet
as he went along. He moved his arms around her and wrapped
her in a sarong-type style.

She was very suspicious, but she couldn't be absolutely sure
the brushing of his hands wasn't necessary under the circumstances, because he was so sober and quick about it.

Then he very efficiently scooped up her clothes and spread
them where the sheet had been on the brace and anchored them
with rocks. It was more than likely because they were so un-
handily small that his hands appeared to linger over her wildly
printed blue and green cotton briefs. What must he think of her
wearing briefs of green and blue under a purple suit! Her sen-
sibilities flinched.

Embarrassed, Peggy stood there, her hair already drying in
the hot dry breeze that caressed her water-cooled body, and she
became aware of how completely exhausted she was. It had
been a long, unusual day, and it was catching up with her. Her
eyes drooped as she yawned.

"You need a nap," Joe decided. "I'll put the mattress over
there by the oak, and you can lie down." He went off to do
that.

Did she dare? One of the things drilled into her from birth
was that, when with a man, one never should lie flat. No matter
what the circumstances, with a date, she should stay sitting up.
Her mother said that to lie down made a woman appear to invite unwanted attentions.

She watched Joe stride barefooted across the sandy, sticky space. His soles must have been made of cast iron, because he didn't have to pick his way. And his muscles must have been iron, too. She found her eyelids grow heavy at the sight of his body so nearly naked.

She decided it would be all right for her to go sit on the mattress and lean against the tree trunk and at least rest. She would not lie down. She did not want to invite his unwanted... She would sit up. Into her mind crept the image of herself sprawled, really rather carelessly, and the sheet coming undone. She *would* sit up.

The day and the swim had so drained her that it was an effort to walk, picking her barefooted way, across to the oak's shade and the mattress. He didn't share her lassitude, but he bent and arranged the mattress, then stood effortlessly and grinned. "There, princess, and there are no peas under it. I cleared them all away."

She needlessly checked the anchoring of her sheet and hoisted it up a trifle more under her arms before she eased down carefully to her clamped-together knees and then curled back to lean against the rough oak bark. It was not comfortable that way. She raised her eyes to Joe to see what he intended to do while she...rested.

He stood there in his red briefs. Her eyes were drawn to his muscles, his hairy chest and flat stomach, and his hands on his hips—and he watched her.

"Thank you. You can run along now." She contrived a very cool look.

He smiled, and his chipped tooth and crinkles were attractions to be added to his hairy chest, his obvious masculinity, and his muscles. "I'm tired, too. You've worked the tail off me all afternoon."

That was an obvious lie. He was bursting with energy. He almost vibrated. She wished she had on very dark sunglasses so her peeking at him would not be so obvious. She licked her lips and replied carefully, "You aren't going to nap on this mattress." But her words did not sound firm enough. "You aren't," she repeated, but those two silly words sounded as if they were questioning.

"Just on the very edge?" His smile widened, amused.

"No." She had to force her lips not to linger in the O position.

"Well," he sighed theatrically. "I suppose I'll just have to lie down here on the sand and the stickery weeds." His eyes seemed to glow as he returned her regard.

She licked her lips again, and then had to begin twice before she could form the words. "The quilt is dry. It only had to be shaken." Her voice must be tired, too, she decided, because it was still breathy, hesitant, and weak, and her arm was exhausted, because she couldn't lift but one finger to give an ineffectual indication in the direction of the quilt which flapped on the rope. He might very easily assume that she was willing to be convinced he should share the mattress. She waited.

He looked at the quilt and then back at her, and his grin was just plain wicked. Then he surprised her. He walked over and lifted the quilt from the rope, folded it, brought it into the shade and busily cleared a space, flipped the quilt out, smoothed it, settled himself down, and apparently went right to sleep!

The bark dug into her back, but the Gulf breeze in the oak leaves soothed her. She scooted down a little, then a little more. She yawned and curled up on her side, and she, too, went to sleep.

Her dreams were erotic, and she became hot and restless. She wakened in a sweat, and found she was lying sprawled rather carelessly. Her sheet had come undone and her breasts were bare; her entire body was shockingly excited. She jerked up her sheet as she realized where she was, and with whom, and she lifted her head to find him, but he wasn't on the quilt.

She sighed in relief. He was somewhere else. She rose up to straighten her wrappings and make herself modest again...and *he was right there next to her on the mattress*! She gasped. His strong, beautifully muscled back was toward her, and he appeared to be fast asleep.

Had he...? Had he been...touching her? Had her dreams...had they really been dreams? She blushed and turned completely scarlet. Her mouth opened and closed. Then her brain told her, It's like Francine said: you're hyper. Relax. What could he have done? If he'd really touched you, you would have wakened then. You didn't. His back is to you. He just preferred to sleep on the mattress instead of on that thin quilt. It's understandable. Why would you think you are so irresistible? He's Henry's friend; he thinks you're Francine. He wouldn't...

But he enjoyed hugging me. He did that and he *purred*!

Purred, her brain asked. Men don't purr. He only held you to stop you from running away. And it's just as well. You had no idea where to go. No plan at all.

But he held me until long after the rest left. He could have let go. He enjoyed it. And his purr made my breasts tingle.

You liked it, too, her brain stated with some impatience.

Peggy moved her legs restlessly, tugging the sheet higher under her armpits, almost cutting off the circulation. He stirred, then he yawned hugely—was it a fake?—and stretched. He moved his strong arms and arched his beautiful back, and the muscles rolled under his tanned skin. Was he deliberately showing off? Then he turned toward her, his nearest knee raised, and his eyes danced.

If he had just awakened why were his eyes so humorous? He looked at her as if she were the one who made him so amused. He said, as if surprised she was awake, "Well, hello!" Did his greeting sound contrived? He went on, "Uh...you were sleeping so tidily in that one corner, I really didn't think you'd mind my using the rest of the mattress. It was just going to waste."

She couldn't think of anything to say. Had he...touched her? What if... They were out there all alone. She blurted, "I wonder when Henry will be here? He'll probably come pretty soon now. I suppose the clothes will be dry. I'll see...." With one arm clamped against her breasts, she locked her knees together and very, very carefully, with excessive stiffness, rose to her feet, and as if a broom handle was down her back she walked carefully over the rough ground to the rope.

She found a man's shirt and some men's walking shorts that were dry. Taking them, she went toward the shack. As she came to the corner of the porch, she peeked back. He was lying on his back, that knee up, his hands under his head, and even from that distance, he appeared pleased. Why?

Keeping track of him out the back window of the shack, she slid out of the sheet and jammed her arms into the sleeves of the all-enveloping shirt. The tails came down to her knees. As she buttoned it, Joe rose from the mattress, which he lifted and carried back to the fence posts. Under the mattress had been a strip of canvas. He went back, shook the sand from it, and flipped the piece over a branch of the oak.

He retrieved his jeans from the windmill and went to the privy. As she put on the walking shorts, she saw him emerge, wearing the jeans, and he came toward the shack. She looked down. Two of her would fit in those shorts. She searched for a tie to hold them up and could find nothing, so she ripped the hem from the top of the sheet. Then she had to find a knife to cut it to a proper length before she threaded it through the belt loops and gathered it around her waist. It was clumsy and bulky, she saw in despair.

Well, so what? She wasn't trying to look attractive for Joe, was she? For her captor? If she looked strange, he would ignore her. No. He wasn't stupid enough to be fooled by ill-fitting clothing. She would need to be careful. She would have to keep him busy. Where *was* Henry?

Of course, Joe undoubtedly wasn't a sex maniac who had brought her here to spend his lusts. If he had intended doing that, he'd had all day for it. There was no way she could have stopped him. Obviously the three roadblockers trusted Joe; he had convinced them she would be safe with him. Was she?

As Joe came in the door she said, "I have to call my parents. They'll be worried." They wouldn't be. Not after that call to the housekeeper. But it was worth a try. She couldn't simply give up.

He raised his eyebrows and inquired with courtesy, "How do you expect to contact them?"

"With a telephone. It's a convenience which people at a distance use to speak with each other."

"And this allows celestial communication? I understood you to say you are an orphan and therefore no one was around to pay ransom."

"Yes..." Never lie unless you can remember your lies, she mentioned to her brain. "Well...uh...foster parents?"

He shook his head.

"Parole supervisor?"

He shook it again.

"Francine?"

He smiled. "You're tricky." He tilted his head. "So you have parents who can pay the ransom. How much should I ask for, or will *I* have to pay, like in 'The Ransom of Red Chief'?"

"Red Chief?"

"O. Henry's story of the nasty brat who drove the kidnappers crazy until they had to negotiate with the father over what *they* had to pay *him* to take the kid back."

She considered replying and finally said, "I'm hungry."

"You *are* lucky! I'm a good cook. And we have just about everything here." He went over to the freezer and took out steaks, French fries, vegetables, bread and a pie.

He took an old metal garbage lid from between the freezer and the refrigerator. He went outside, set it in a cleared space by the pump and filled it with wood. Then he lit the wood. He pumped some water from the well until it ran clear, then put the frozen steaks in the pan of water to thaw. Back inside the shack he lifted a trap door in the floor and removed an electric oven. "We can't make it too easy for thieves," he said to Peggy.

He plugged the oven into a socket, put the pie inside it, and went about the making of the meal. Peggy gathered the clothes from the line and folded them. Then she set the table on the porch, and Joe carried out the two chairs. She couldn't resist saying, "How nice Faraday doesn't actually sit at the table, since there are just two chairs. He doesn't sit at the table, does he?''

Joe looked at her and replied slowly, ''I'd like sharing a chair with you.''

She turned away and had to swallow at the thought of being jammed against him on a chair, touching him, feeling him breathe.... She snatched up some shears and gathered a bouquet of weeds whose grain heads and greens contrasted in an interesting way and put them in a jar to be used as a centerpiece.

Companionably, Joe told her, ''Henry bought this place so he could come here when things got to be too much. Too many phone calls, too many confused people, too much pressure. He has several places like this. And he lends them to people he thinks could benefit from the stillness...the change.'' He leaned his head back and looked around as if *he* owned it all and relished it. ''We'll go fishing tomorrow.''

''You're assuming Henry won't get here tonight.''

''...If Henry doesn't come tonight,'' Joe added dutifully.

But while Peggy listened for the sound of a car or a pickup, Joe never seemed to expect anyone.

If Faraday expected Henry, he hid it well. He sat around some, but mostly he just lolled on his side, blinking his eyes and yawning. She had seen the dog walk twice. To the pond and back when they swam.

Just then he heaved himself to his feet and woofed as if it took great effort. Joe fed him. But Joe put the tin plate by Faraday so the dog didn't actually have to move.

The food disappeared from the tin plate, and the dog just looked mournfully at Joe until Joe went over, rinsed off the plate under the pump, filled it with water, and returned it to the dog...who drank from it. Then Faraday lay back down and rested.

Joe washed his hands and began to wrap food in foil to go on the grill.

''Doesn't that dog ever do anything?''

''Well, you see, he's a registered stud,'' Joe explained, and Peggy was sorry she had asked. ''He has to rest up a lot.'' He smiled at the dog, who blinked modestly. "He's choosy, too. He won't service just any bitch. It has to be true love—no matter how brief."

Why didn't he drop it? She asked quickly, "What kind of fish are caught here?" in order to change the subject.

"Catfish, sunfish…" He was buttering and sprinkling garlic salt on chunks of French bread. He went on, "There was one bitch who insisted, but he didn't like her. She nipped him, and he turned his back and scraped dirt over her with his hind feet." Joe laughed.

She persisted with the conversational red herring. "Do you fly cast or use a bent pin?"

"Once Faraday got up on a chair and sat there while a bitch begged and whined. He ignored her because she hadn't paid."

"What sort of bait do you use?" Peggy babbled on.

He grinned at her and his eyes were as wicked as they could be. He asked softly, "What kind would you like?"

Her eyes must have crossed and her tongue tangled up, because with all the diverse chatter, she wasn't sure they were both thinking about the same thing. Her body went oddly still, and goose bumps skittered over the surface of her skin. Her lips became very dry—from the Gulf breeze—and she had to lick them twice.

His eyelids came down halfway in sensual awareness, as if he knew exactly what she was feeling, and it pleased him, and his own tongue freshened his own lips. Then his lower lip tightened, as if he had to stop a smug smile.

He couldn't possibly know what her body felt. She knew that, in looking around and taking only occasional peeks at him, to him she appeared cool and indifferent. Why did she experience this amazing reaction to him? Before she had ever even seen his face there in the elevator that very first time, her body's response to his had been sensational, and at that time he hadn't yet smiled at her and exposed his chipped tooth, or touched her, or even spoken to her.

What on earth was happening to her? How could it be? She had only met him that morning!

It had to be hunger. Once she was fed she would be okay again. She did feel a little faint and disoriented. And one did feel that way when one was very hungry. She hadn't eaten since breakfast, at about ten thirty. She'd had that Popsicle....

"Where did you get the lime Popsicles? They're very scarce."

"Henry has them made up special."

"Henry would."

"He likes all the best things."

"Yes." She knew Henry did.

"And so do I."

She shot a look at him, wondering if that had any hidden meaning. Would he make a play for her just because he thought she was Francine? Did he feel competitive with Henry? Would he try to break them up, keeping "Francine" here alone with him to make Henry jealous?

What would he do when he found out that his scheme was misdirected and she was not Francine? What would *she* do? How was she to survive this interlude with such an attractive man who was obviously attracted to her, too—or pretended to be? What a mess. "I'm not Francine."

He smiled over at her tolerantly. "How do you like your steak?"

"Cooked." The sun was going down. It was very peaceful. The crickets stirred. The mosquitoes would be next. "Do you have any mosquito repellent?"

"In the truck cab, right behind the seat."

She walked over to the truck, her bare feet picking their choosy way, and she opened the passenger door. She reached back and felt around blindly—and felt another rope. There was also a tool box, and her wrist brushed against a small metal container that clung to the underside of the seat.

Curious, she tugged at it and found it was magnetic. A hidden key? Her fingers got excited, and her breathing quickly followed suit.

Not believing her luck, she detached the box and pulled it into view. It *was* an extra key to the truck! She straightened a bit and peeked at Joe from the corners of her eyes. He was fooling with the steaks, completely unsuspecting. Could she? Could she...escape?

She would just go around the truck, get in, lock the door...and leave. She sneaked the lock button down on the passenger side and the sound of it locking reverberated clear to the foothills of the Rockies. She closed her eyes, waiting for him to storm over.

He didn't. She stole a glance over the sill of the window; he must not have heard the lock. Guilt did that: it made sounds seem exceptionally loud.

She swung the door closed in a very businesslike manner. Then, with the jerky movements of elaborate casualness, she circled the truck and needlessly called out, "It must have slid over to the other side," as she pretended she couldn't find the repellent, and that gave her the excuse to get into the truck on the driver's side.

He smiled at her. Just the nicest smile. Then he went right back to cooking her dinner. It was really rather rude to leave with all that food prepared. He probably liked his steak raw— thrown through the bars of his cage—and hers would be well-done, and he couldn't eat hers that way. It would go to waste.

What on earth was she thinking? Here she had been womannapped and brought to this isolated place by a handsome stranger, and night was approaching, and who knew what could happen there, at night, in the dark!

A thrill started at her toes and suffused her entire body. She hesitated. She actually hesitated! There on the verge of escaping, the thought of spending the night with that stranger had made her hesitate. Still, it *would* be interesting to see what would happen. What would he do if they were alone out there in that cramped one-room cabin, with only one bed, in the middle of such isolation...?

Throttling her imagination, she stepped quickly into the cab of the pickup, slammed the door, locked it, furiously rolled up the window, and inserted the key in the ignition. Her heart was in her mouth. She was going to escape. Again she hesitated as she took one last look at Joe.

He was placidly turning the steaks, and he wasn't even look-ing in her direction. The slamming door hadn't caught his attention.

Did he believe he had already enslaved her? That she was so bemused by his charm and body that she couldn't leave? Did he consider himself so irresistible? He didn't *care* that she was getting away, and he hadn't...they hadn't...he hadn't even kissed her!

She turned the key, and the starter motor ground. She turned it again and pumped the gas pedal. She tried again. It would not start.

She looked at the truck hood with indignation and ground the motor again. Then her eyes caught a movement by her door, so her head whipped around, and there stood Joe.

He stood there looking courteous, biting his lower lip as if in concern at the unresponding truck motor, but she knew he was keeping from laughing. How rude of him.

As their eyes met again he smiled in a very friendly way, as if she hadn't been trying to get away. She turned off the key and sat there trying to decide what to do. She would just stay there in the truck and be safe...from him. She looked at him again.

He wasn't the least bit threatening. Not in a harmful way. However, as a male who was excessively attractive, he was an-other matter entirely.

He reached into his pocket, pulled out a key ring...and un-locked the door. She sat there. He opened the door and said very kindly, "That was a brilliant try. You sure could have fooled me. And thinking to say the repellent had slipped over to the other side! That was a stroke of genius!"

"Oh, shut up."

He laughed.

Four

Silent and sulking, Peggy sat woodenly at the table on the sagging porch while Joe cheerfully whistled as he finished organizing their dinner. When he had finished with the steaks, he pumped a pan of water and splashed it over the coals. She blurted a protest. "I like seeing the fire when it's dark." But he ignored her as he busily carried their plates to the table and sat down.

"Why did you have to put it out?" Peggy tried to quarrel. "It'll be so dark soon, we won't be able to see. You'll have to put on the headlights."

He replied reasonably, "Although we have electricity to keep the freezer and refrigerator working, at night we have no lights at all."

They would be there—alone in the dark. A roll of sensation started in the pit of her stomach and slid slowly in a loop throughout her torso, fascinating her, weakening her knees, and freezing her spine as it immobilized her face—doubtlessly leaving her looking cool and indifferent...and in control.

He chewed, swallowed, licked his firm masculine lips, then said to her, "Honey, it really is dangerous around here. Besides the snakes and gila monsters, and the dog packs, we have coyotes, the kind who smuggle in illegal aliens, and we have drug runners. They're exceptionally dangerous. We have to be careful. We're very isolated here, and we don't want to draw attention to ourselves."

"There are people who live in this isolation." She gave him an aloof look.

"Yes. Fully alert, and with caution."

"You make it sound...risky." She began to pay attention.

"Anything is."

"Then why live out here?"

"Why risk anything? There are pluses." He smiled at her in the last of the sunshine as the sun began to sink out of sight in the west.

Risk? Speaking of risk, why was he risking keeping her there with him? She could bring very serious charges against him. And what did he do with his time that he could so casually keep her there? He had wasted a full day on this capture. Did he owe Henry a favor? Why?

In the gathering night, she restrained her curiosity. Getting chatty would be too friendly, and she wanted to keep the restraint between them. To be friendly now might seem welcoming. Not that he had given any real indication that he would welcome any advances from her. Though he had purred when he held her close to him that time. She peeked at him. He was probably thinking about ravishing her.

He was watching the sun set, and he remarked idly, "It's said the sun rises and sets, but actually the horizon rises at night and sinks in the morning." He cast a glance her way. "Does that give you a feeling of insecurity? To know we're on this rolling ball wobbling along out here in space?"

She looked at him in the last of the sun's light. It wasn't what the world was doing or why that made her feel insecure and not in control. She could handle what the world did and the fact there was no string holding up this blue ball they all rode on.

What she could not handle was her reaction to Joseph Richards.

What did she mean she couldn't handle it? Of course she could! She was a mature woman of twenty-two, with a degree in elementary education, and she would begin substitute teaching that very fall. She was going to inspire whole generations of children into becoming the leaders of tomorrow. She would be instrumental in saving the world.

But what was she going to do about tonight? About Joseph Richards? What if he said, "I don't want to sleep in the truck. I'm going to sleep in the shack with you, in that bed, and I'm going to make mad passionate love to you?" What *would* she say...besides yes?

The sun slipped out of sight over the rising horizon and it was dark. Very dark. "It's dark," she told him.

"After a time the stars will give us plenty of light." He moved in his chair, and she was electrified. He was making his move! But he was simply shifting position.

She understood how a taut violin string felt after being plucked; it shimmered and hummed, very agitated. That was the way she felt. She felt agitated, as if all her nerves were shimmering and humming, along with several explicit places inside her body. She shot out of her chair and announced, "I'm going for a walk."

"Honey, it's too dark for walking." He used a reasonable tone. "You could break your neck." In the night his voice was low and soft, sinfully lazy and suggestive—as if he knew better things to do than take a walk.

He wasn't having any trouble being alone out there with her. If he knew how she reacted to him, wouldn't he be frightened? Of course not. He would more than likely say, "Well, I could *try* to fit you into my schedule of women."

What on earth could be the matter with her? He must have sneaked a powerful aphrodisiac into her food. Mixed with the salt.

"I'll...I'll...I'll go swimming!" she blurted. Perhaps that would counteract whatever spell she was under, and she would get so tired she would be able to sleep.

How could she possibly sleep? Lying there on that curlicued bed that looked as if it had spent its best days in a brothel! She would be languorous and exhausted...and defenseless.

Just then he said, "That would be nice," as if he had heard her thoughts!

She went, "Eeeep," like some trapped mouse. "Wh-what do you mean?"

"Swimming." He sounded puzzled.

And well he should be puzzled. She was acting like an idiot. She had to get control of herself. She took a deep, calming breath.

"It's dark enough to go skinny dipping." There was humor in his voice. He undoubtedly had cat's eyes and could see in this pitch blackness.

"No!" Peggy denied that sharply. "We will not swim..." What word was she to use? Unclothed? Naked? The thought of his body naked almost unwomaned her. Maybe overwomaned her.

"Come on, it'll be fun," he coaxed, and she gasped. But he went on, "It'll help settle our stomachs after that big meal."

His mind wasn't running amok the way hers was. He was talking about swimming. He was being perfectly logical and courteous. It was her unbridled mind that was making his words sound lascivious. She was being unreasonably stupid. Francine was right. She *was* warped over men, but not the way Francine thought. No, it was the very opposite.

No other man had ever affected her in this way. She could never remember any man's body drawing her eyes the way Joe's did. Not one had made her fingers itch to explore as his did, or made her so conscious of her own mouth, or her breasts, or her movements, or of her own body. The aphrodisiac had to have been in the lime Popsicle.

Well, maybe not. She had been conscious of him at the Hilton. He must have shaken the dust of some strange sex-heightening powder on her when he first removed his hat on the elevator. She was becoming paranoid.

After twenty-two years of a perfectly orderly life, she was coming unhinged. She tried to remember if she had ever heard of any strange behavior gossiped over at family reunions. Of course, if her whole family was this way, there would be no gossip. They would all consider this kind of behavior normal.

Since her daddy was an army career officer, and they had been stationed in other states and foreign countries, Peggy really didn't know her relations very well. But she concocted a sample discussion of the family trait: "Cisco going through the Phase yet?" and the reply: "I think he got a double dose, what with us being cousins."

While her mind was buzzing along its strange new pathways, Joe had taken their dishes, put them into the pan, and pumped water over them so they could soak. Then he straightened and stretched and yawned—and she realized that she could see him.

The starlight even cast shadows. The sky was clear, and God had lavishly strewn the blue night-velvet with swirls of diamonds. It was breathtaking. She stepped from the porch and allowed her eyes to feast on Joe there in the starlight. With it so dark, he wouldn't be able to tell she was watching him. She stared at the marvelous male silhouette of him.

When he lazily turned her way, she tilted her head as if she had been examining the spectacular display of stars, and it was too dark for him to see her blush.

He reached out his hand and said, "Let's go." She unhesitatingly put her own into his strong, hard hand before she realized he only meant to swim.

"What if Henry comes?"

"Either we'll hear the truck or he'll hear us splashing."

When her tender feet slowed their progress to the pond, he lifted her into his arms and carried her. He did it effortlessly, not hurrying or even breathing hard. He must rope cows and flip calves in order to develop the muscles she felt under her hands; he could carry her so easily.

She became a bit light-headed. She was no longer hungry, so she decided it was the height. Height? Now, really, Margaret. Three feet off the ground? Be sensible.

"What do you do for a living?" she inquired, and her voice came out soft.

"You getting interested in me?" His own voice was deep and filled with teasing.

"Of course not. It's your...muscles." How gauche she sounded. Like some simpering flirt. Ohhhh, you great big handsome man! Good grief!

"I'm...between jobs right now."

He was a drifter. Here today and gone tomorrow. Someone who loved and then moved on. She would be a fool to get involved with him. Involved with him? Who had asked her?

When they reached the windmill's concrete base he set her on her feet but did not move away. She knew he was going to kiss her and held still. He asked, "Want some help with your buttons?"

"No," she replied in a tiny voice. She looked up at him there in the starlight, at the shadow cast by his eyelashes, at his perfectly formed lips, at the way the slight breeze moved his hair over his forehead.

Her hand came up to her chest as she almost reached up to allow her fingers to bury themselves in his hair and smooth it back. She jerked away from him and stepped down on the embedded bench to dive into the pond—and she dived right out of her humungous walking shorts! She hung there in the water wearing only that big shirt. Well, it was dark.

And my God, it was cold! That should take his mind off sex. She set out strongly to swim in the magic pool filled with a sky of reflected stars. Actually, why did she think his mind was on sex? He had made no overt move.

Outside of purring as he held her plastered against him with *three other men around*, he had made no move at all. *Had* he touched her as she slept on the mattress under the oak? She had never had dreams quite like that....

The sound of his strokes overtook her, and he loomed beside her as she began to swim back toward the windmill. "At night," he told her, "the alligators come out of the mud and swim in the pond." His teeth flashed white in the darkness.

That stopped her dead in the water, and for a split second her heart jumped into her mouth. But if it *was* true, then he would not be in the pond. "How nice of you to offer your body as an alternative to mine."

"Honey, no alligator is going to take tough-hided Joe Richards over tender, delicious Francine."

"I am not Francine."

He ignored her interruption. "I love to swim at night, but I've always been afraid of them. Even alligators can get hungry enough to eat what's handy. But with you here, and so deliciously tasty, I'm safe."

"You beast!"

"They...*gotcha*!" he roared, and with his hands suddenly clamped around her waist, he jerked her under the water.

She screamed in pure terror as she went down, and he had to push her immediately back to the surface, where she choked and coughed and sputtered. He held her afloat as she kept a stranglehold on him, trying to climb up him and out of the water. She was furious, and he laughed...but then she cried.

He was appalled. "Aw, honey, I didn't mean to really scare you. Come on now. It's okay. Don't cry."

It had been a long, nerve-racking day. She had been on an emotional high—one way or the other—all day, and she was just too strung out. And who knew what really might be lurking in that deep, isolated, farm pond? The Loch Ness monster?

She pushed herself away from him to thrash in barely controlled nerves over to the bench, and he followed. She grasped the edge of the bench to lift herself from the now scary pond, and he put a helpful hand on her bottom and shoved her up.

It wasn't the shove that lifted her so quickly to the bench so much as it was the feel of his hard hand on her bare bottom; the shock of that made her jump up on the bench like a scalded cat.

She stepped up to the cement and stood there shivering, with the water running off her. She pulled down the wet shirt to her knees, and it clung to her completely.

He came out of the water almost as easily as she had, and with it as dark as it was, she did not turn away, but he had on briefs. He stepped to the top of the bank and stood beside her, putting his big hand on her shoulder—enclosing the whole of it. "You okay?" He had to stoop a little in order to peer into her face.

"That was a beastly thing to do!" She found that her lower lip trembled on its own and her eyes peeked up at him in a perfectly outrageous way. She straightened up and took control of herself. She tilted her head back and looked him straight in the eye as she went on, "Saying there were alligators in the pond and scaring me that way!"

"Now, honey, you ought to know Texas doesn't have alligators. Alligators only live in Florida and the sewers of New York City."

She was jittery from the cold, the fright, and from her long day. Her teeth chattered, and she began to shiver harder.

"Here." His voice was low and tender. "Take off that wet shirt and put mine on. It's dry."

"I...don't..."

"It's okay. It's dark. I can't see."

Yeah. Sure. But she was so cold.... That shirt clung to her like ice. She turned her back and began to fumble with the wet buttonholes, but he took hold of the bottom of her shirt and simply skinned it off over her head, and she was standing there stark naked.

It was a minute before anything happened. She quit shivering, oddly enough, and she did not move, but though she refused to turn her head, her eyes strained as she tried to see behind her. It was silent except for the breeze touching the weeds and the few sleepy crickets.

She could hear his breath, and her skin knew he was close behind her; then she heard him swallow before he said, "Here," in a tender, husky, very low voice. He put his soft dry denim shirt against her back and held it there until she realized he meant for her to put her arms into the sleeves.

He was taller than she and could see down over her shoulder. The thought warmed her considerably, and then she was the one who swallowed rather noisily and licked her lips and had to leave her mouth open a bit so she could breathe a little.

She tried to make her trembling fingers button the shirt, but they could only fumble. He turned her around and wrapped his strong arms around her and held her close to him. "I didn't mean to scare you that way. I never in this world thought you'd believe me. I'm as sorry as I can be."

She allowed herself the exquisite pleasure of his comforting. She lay against his damp, bare, hairy chest and sighed as she relaxed, her wet hair sending rivulets down her back under his dry shirt. She heard herself give a little sniff. Had she done that? Surely not.

"Aw, honey, if you cry it'll tear my heart out."

"I'm not crying," she hastened to reassure him. "It's just...I'm not. You see... It's okay. I understand. I'm not scared now." He loosened his arms. Well, damn.

"We need to dry your hair."

"Yes," she agreed vaguely. She wasn't paying any attention at all. She was going over the facts and reminding herself that she had only been acquainted with him for one day. How shocking.

Her behavior was very strange There are amateur virgins, who either haven't been tested or who just aren't sure, but then there was Margaret Indiana Dillon, who had looked the situation over and knew that sex was for the birds and the bees. It had been a clear-eyed, levelheaded, adult decision.

By that point Joe had picked her up and was carrying her over to the shack as if that was the way men and women always moved from one place to another: with the him carrying the her. Since she was wearing nothing but a shirt, this seemed an excruciatingly intimate way to travel, with her body across the front of his muscular chest and hard, flat stomach that way, and with his arms around her and holding her like that.

He had very carefully caught the tail of the shirt under her thighs so her bare bottom was not waving in the breeze, but they both knew now that she didn't have on her underwear. It was an embarrassing situation for a professional virgin.

And now they were arriving at that one-room, one-bed shack. She became even stiffer—if that were possible—and her mind went skittering around, looking for a way to solve things. Henry had not yet shown up. "Henry isn't here." Her mouth spilled out the thought without checking with her brain. Why was she reminding him that they were out there all alone?

Joe stood there, holding her easily, and looked around the starlit expanse, as if Henry's pickup could be tucked away behind some crooked cedar fence post or clump of grasses. "No, by golly, he isn't!"

"I'm sure he'll still come tonight. I'll just sit on the porch and wait."

Was he courteous? No, he was not. He laughed a deliciously wicked laugh.

She huffed. "I don't see anything funny about my sitting on the porch and waiting."

"I know you don't, honey, and that's why it's so amusing."

Faraday wuffed a minimal sound to remind them that he had been stalwartly guarding the place while they had been away frivolously cavorting in the pond, having a good time and leaving him there all by himself.

Peggy wiggled to be released, but Joe's arms tightened as he suddenly asked, "Do you speak Spanish?"

Readily she replied, "*Gracias*," mispronouncing it as "gracious." Then she added flippantly, "Tortilla, enchilada, tostada..."

"Any conversational Spanish?"

"I took French." Her dad had been stationed in Paris while she was in high school and she had continued the subject in college.

"French? How logical. So many Texans speak French."

"Actually—" she was serious "—a great many speak Spanish.... You were joshing me!" she accused.

"Never! Quit wiggling. If I set you down here you'll get your toes all sandy and get the sand on the floor and in the sheets." He carried her to the porch and set her down there. Then he reached to rub Faraday's head. "I'll get you an ice cream bar for your late-night snack. How's that?" Then he asked Peggy, "Would you like another lime Popsicle?"

"Uh, no. Thanks anyway." More aphrodisiac, no doubt.

"Sure?" he asked hospitably. "Henry has boxes of them." When she shook her head he added, "Think I'll have one." And he went inside to root around in the freezer.

Good heavens! If he ate one and it really did contain an aphrodisiac, and he became affected, and as susceptible as she felt, it could only lead to disaster.

She quickly slipped inside the shack, where the freezer light reflected up into Joe's beautiful face, and she was forced to say casually, "Why don't you just have an ice cream bar with Faraday."

"Selfish, huh. Want all the limes to yourself?"

She snatched that idea. "Yes."

He chuckled and shook his head. He took out an ice cream bar and closed the lid, and it was again dark in the shack. "Well, okay. There ought to be enough Popsicles for you there for our first month, anyway."

"*Month!*"

"Henry isn't here." Silhouetted against the window, he spread his arms out in the dark room. "He may never show up. He may have found a less tiresome female and decided to just let you sit a while and fret."

"I am not Francine," she told him again in a level voice.

"You keep saying that, honey, but you were wearing a purple suit and driving a red car. How many women do you know who would do that on the same day, coming out of the Hilton in downtown San Antonio?" His tone was reasonable.

"I am not Francine, and Henry won't give two hoots about where I am, and I want to go home."

"When we called Henry, we called your parents, too, and said you were taking a little holiday."

"You called Francine's parents?"

"Everybody knows what's going on, and there's no need for you to worry about a thing. You leave it all to me. I'll take care of you. I know what I'm doing." He crossed the lighter rectangle of the open door as he went to the peg and took his hat from it and put it on. "Lie down on the bed and wait for Henry. I'd rather you weren't on the porch. You make a delectable outline for someone nosing around. I'm going to step out for a while and check around the area to see what's going on. Of course, I'll sleep in the truck, so I probably won't see you until morning. Close your eyes and rest, honey. If Henry shows up, you'll hear soon enough."

"You're leaving me here alone?"

"No, the valiant Faraday will block the door and anyone trying to enter will stumble over him and he'll complain so much, you can sneak out the window."

"The windows are too narrow for me to get out of them."

"True. But I'd hear Faraday and I'd be back just in the nick of time to save you. Want me to tuck you in?"

"No. Thanks anyway."

"How about a good-night kiss?"

"No. You're probably all sticky from the ice cream bar."

Halfway through her sentence he was already laughing. "You could...lick it off," he offered.

She didn't reply but went over and sat on the edge of the bed, which squeaked in protest. She instantly stood up.

His chuckle sounded low and very amused. "At least I'll know if you're sleeping tonight as I lie crunched up on that miserable, narrow, short cab seat."

"You could sleep on the bed of the truck."

"It's as hard as your heart." He had to put his foot against the bottom of the screen door to shove it open as he moved an inert Faraday over enough so that he could squeeze out the door. Faraday did not make a sound.

She went over to the door and said accusingly, "Faraday didn't make any sound at all when you went out this door!"

"Well, he's asleep." Joe stated the obvious.

"And what if someone came..."

"Like a dog pack?" His voice was unsteady. "If Faraday didn't make one sound, I bet I'd sure enough hear you, honey." And just like that, he was gone.

She went from window to window to door, and she couldn't see any sign of him. What if he just...left? She stood there in the quiet night and thought about that. She certainly had enough to eat. And water. She could live there for a year...if no one came along and wanted the food or the shack or her. She could live there in the lovely, quiet beauty of that place...and it wouldn't be any fun at all without Joe.

She went over to the freshly made up, very tidy bed and sat on the quilt. It was strange the impact Joe had had on her. Even before she had seen his face, there had been that strong, magnetic current between them. At least she had felt it. Had he?

She got off the squeaky bed and groped through the stack of clean clothes on the table and found a towel—and her underwear. Then she sat back down on the bed and dried her hair slowly. The collar of his shirt was damp on her back from her wet hair. She could change the shirt; there were others in the stack. She hugged his shirt around her and found herself wishing it was Joe she was hugging. That was sobering.

With her hair almost dry, she cleaned her feet with the towel; then she lay down on top of the quilt to wait for Henry to come. Surely Francine would send Henry for her? If not Henry, someone should come for her. Francine knew she was with Joe.

Who would deliberately leave her out there in this isolated place with that devastating man? Why would Francine be so cruel as to rub her nose into temptation in this way. Actually her nose would be rubbing in Joe. What a perfectly thrilling idea! She eased over sideways to change her thoughts and that was the last she knew.

Since Faraday didn't make a sound, she didn't hear the door being quietly opened, nor did she waken when she was lifted so the quilt could be pulled up over her. She only sighed when he sat carefully on the squeaky bed and swung his legs under the quilt with her.

She murmured and wiggled closer when he took her into his arms, and her lips were soft as rose petals as he gently kissed her, taking her quick breaths into his mouth as he smiled in the darkness.

She wakened to a snore. She had slept heavily, but she knew instantly that she was in a strange bed. The snore was closer than her parents' room. It was very close. It was next to her, and the arm of the snorer was lying heavily across her waist.

Very, very carefully she peeked back over her shoulder and was not too surprised to see that it was Joe. The quilt was casually draped low on his naked stomach; he was heavily asleep. He rolled over on his back, his arm moving off her. He breathed deeply, and then his bubbling snore gurgled in his throat. He had such a nice snore. One of the comforting ones. She smiled.

Good heavens, Margaret, get up and get out of here! Now's your chance! Up and at 'em. But each minute movement brought a creaking protest from the old springs under the mattress. And as she stood up, his snore stopped. He moved restlessly, and one knee rose.

She was trapped against the wall by the bottom of the ornate bedstead and the sleeping man. She attempted to step carefully across the bottom of the bed, but each movement brought the springs' renewed protest.

Finally she decided to use the bedstead's curlicues as silent stepping-stones across the end of the bed and past his feet to the floor.

It wasn't easy. The openings in the bedstead were at different heights, and some were very small. The top of the bedstead almost reached to the low ceiling, so she couldn't simply climb over it. She set herself to her task, and of necessity her back was to Joe.

"What are you doing?" His deep voice froze her like a fly on a screen.

"Eeee!" she went.

"*Now* what are you so flustered about?" He sounded just a bit cranky. Of course it was very early. Barely daylight. "Are you trying to escape again?"

"Oh, no," she lied.

"You woke up and found me here, and you've panicked."

"Oh, no."

"Why can't you trust me?"

"Trust you!" That obviously astonished her, and she turned around to step onto the bed; then she had to turn back and work her other foot out of a curlicue. "Trust you?" The words seemed to fascinate her.

"Yes." He was a little indignant.

"You snatched me away, and you're holding me prisoner, and you have the gall to ask me to trust you?" She was warming up.

"Well." He had both knees up and his arms folded behind his head. "Other than kidnapping you and holding you against your will, what have I done to make you distrust me?"

"That's not sufficient?" She gestured widely, standing there in his long-tailed shirt and barefooted.

He frowned and said grudgingly, "I suppose I can see where that might give you pause. But what else have I done that'd make you want to get away from me?" He definitely sounded cross. "I'm not very receptive to argument, remember. I've quit smoking and my temper's chancy."

"I...I...I have to go outside."

"It's hardly morning. Come back to bed."

"I will not!" She was quite indignant.

"If you had one ounce of compassion, you'd make love with me and calm me down."

She gasped and couldn't seem to exhale.

"A man who's quit smoking is tense and disagreeable, and any woman would recognize that and help him out. But what do you do? Here I finally get to sleep and can rest and relax, and you hop up and climb up and down the bedstead. Have you quit, too?"

"I was *trying* to keep the bed from squeaking."

He moved his big body and deliberately made the springs protest. "Come here," he said, and he smiled at her.

"Now, Joe..." she began.

"Now's as good a time as any. Come here and let's make this bed sing."

"You...shock me." Then she said in a censuring way, "How could you do that to Henry, if you think I'm Francine?"

"If you're not Francine, where's the harm?"

"I'm—"

"You're...what?"

Now how was she supposed to say she wasn't Francine when she was trapped there by that damned bedstead and that wickedly attractive man? All she would have to do was say she wasn't Francine and he could take that as agreeing that she wanted to make love with him to help him relax—since he had quit smoking.

Make love just because he was tense from not smoking? How romantically could a man proposition a woman? "Hey, I'm tense"? She looked down her nose and her temper flared.

That made him laugh. "You are the most interesting woman I've ever met."

Biting off the words in a quelling way, she retorted, "I'm a very ordinary, mature woman. I will not 'sleep' with you to ease your tension, and I am not Francine."

"Honey—"

"And you can stop calling me 'honey.'"

"Then what should I call you? Darling?"

"You may call me Miss Dillon!" she snapped.

But that only made him laugh again.

Five

———

Lying there in the rumpled bed, Joe stretched his arms up, his muscles rolling in lazy power, and he smiled sleepily at Peggy, who stood like a pinned butterfly against the bedstead. In a reasonable way he informed her, "Distractions are important. When a man quits smoking, it's just plain hell. The first time I set eyes on you, I knew you'd be distracting. You are just the prettiest little thing. Just looking at you makes my...toes wiggle." He smiled wickedly. "Come on down off that bedstead and distract me."

Peggy stood with both hands on her thighs, holding down the shirttails in case some errant wind came bursting into the shack and lifted the cloth, and she blushed. Could she step across his feet modestly? There she was and...and she heard a rooster crow!

"I heard a rooster!" she exclaimed. Joe looked blank. "A *barnyard* rooster!" she elaborated.

He lifted one hand and motioned slowly, dismissing such an idea. "It's probably a wild one. A wild Texas bush rooster." He nodded as he agreed with himself. "There aren't any houses anywhere near us for barnyard roosters."

Would he lie? Of course he would. He was holding her against her will, so one lie more or less wouldn't bother him. She listened closely to see if she could tell the direction of the wild Texas rooster's crow, but she had no idea. She needed to get outside and listen. "If you would excuse me," she told him primly, "I'd like to go outside."

He lay there looking carelessly attractive and asked, "Are you sure you want to leave me lying here all wound up and needful? Are you that cruel, honey?"

"Don't call me honey. I just told you that."

"Now, you *know* I can't be calling you 'Miss Dillon' after sleeping with you. That's just ridiculous."

"I did not sleep with you!"

"Well, after sharing a bed." He willingly corrected the wordage, but what he came up with sounded worse. "I gotta call you 'honey' 'cause we both know Francine belongs to another man." He drawled it out, and his tone was filled with humor.

"Let me go." She was suddenly very earnest. "This is a dumb thing for a grown man to be doing—baby-sitting me. Take me back to my car and pull it out and let me go."

"Now, honey, I have to keep you here. But I'll do whatever it takes to make you as comfortable as possible. And if you should want to fool around then...I'd be willing to endure." He smiled. "Try me."

"I really need to go outside."

He watched her.

She lifted her chin. "Move so that I may get off the bed."

He moved slowly, carefully. He drew air in through his teeth. He wasn't kidding. He *was* in pain.

"What's the matter?" she asked sharply.

"I fell off a horse last week. I'm okay. I'm just a little slow getting started in the mornings." He grinned at her. "What I need is a good, sweet, slow massage."

"How did you fall off a horse?" Her brain rejected the thought of massaging him, and her fingers went behind her to cling to the curlicued bedstead instead of reaching out and petting the curly wisps on his chest, before rubbing the prickles on his jaw and hurrying up higher to the coarse silk of his hair.

She was mesmerized by where her fingers wanted to go next, when he interrupted by saying, "Rodeo."

His slow straightening and careful movements recalled her to their place in the conversation. She entered on cue and asked, "You ride the circuit?"

"On occasion. I know it's a dumb thing to do, falling off that...*precious* horse." He straightened fully, his eyes squinting just a little; then he held his hand out to help her down from the bed. She said a breathy, "Thank you." His red briefs were all that marred the lovely symmetry of his gorgeous masculine body.

Distracted by him, Peggy pawed through the stacked, clean laundry several times before she remembered why she was doing that, and she finally settled on her now-sleeveless purple suit. She gave him a quick look from the sides of her eyes as she went out the screen door and around the back to the privy. It was set some distance away, because the well was in the front yard of the shack.

When she returned, dressed, Joe had started a fire in the garbage lid. He was bare-chested, wearing pants, boots, and his Stetson, of course. He smiled a welcome and handed her a brush. She had finger-combed the worst of the tangles, so it wasn't difficult to smooth her hair.

He watched her; then he gave her a red bandanna to put over her hair to keep it under control and give her some protection from the sun. Red...with that purple...? She put it on.

"Since you're my guest, I'll do the cooking."

"Guest?"

"Right." He nodded emphatically. "Honored guest."

"A guest has the option of leaving."

"I *said* I'd take you home, honey. Just not right now." He went back to laying strips of bacon in the big black iron skillet.

Peggy went inside to find the rumpled bed unmade. Joe could cook, but he couldn't make beds? Or perhaps he still figured on enticing her back into it?

She had to get away. She couldn't just give up and wait for her inevitable seduction. She had to escape. She was not a victim.

But her hand reached down on its own accord to caress the rumpled pillow that had held Joe's head. She was reluctant to smooth it and take away the indication that he had slept there beside her. She sighed, exasperated with herself, and put that hand on her forehead for a minute; then she briskly straightened, smoothed the bed, and snapped it into order, hiding the pillows under the top of the quilt.

Although she realized she had to get away, she needed shoes desperately. She sneaked one cupboard open and found canned goods, then closed it and opened the one on the other side of the window in the east wall. It was filled with shelves, and the shelves were filled with all sorts of things...some clothes, but no shoes that would fit her.

She needed something she could walk on over the uneven ground. Moccasins would be perfect, or something like them.... Her eyes fell on the two purple sleeves she had ripped out of her suit jacket.

She could pull those on over her feet and tie them on with strips from the other end of the sheet she had torn up to hold up the shorts she had dived out of last night. She had no qualms about misusing anything at hand. She was a prisoner.

A guest had to be considerate of her host's possessions, but that sort of conduct wasn't required of prisoners. She was free of all considerations and restrictions. She could do what needed to be done in order to escape. Her conscience soothed, she stepped outside to the porch, and demurely began to set the table.

The way she had it figured, she would appear docile and resigned, and she would work the tail off Joe and exhaust him so fully that he would have to take a nap. Then she would wait until he was asleep and sneak into the shack, wrap her feet and get away.

All she had to do was follow the track until she came to her car.... But the car was still stuck in quicksand. What would she do then? Walk back to the highway and hitchhike to civilization?

Who would pick her up on the highway? Her imagination—gained by her association with Francine—began to ferment and perk. She envisioned all sorts of ghastly encounters that ran horrifyingly through her mental vision in full color and stereophonic sound, which consisted mostly of her screams.

She could not walk out to the highway and chance such disaster. She looked at Joe, who represented disaster of another sort.

He had busily added reconstituted dried milk to prepared pancake mix and was shaking it. The griddle next to the frying pan was hot and waiting. He poured a string of small blobs of batter onto the griddle; then he began breaking eggs into the hot bacon grease in the skillet.

Pancakes *and* eggs? That was entirely too much food. She gathered another bouquet of weeds to grace their breakfast table and noted that Faraday was lying with his chin on one paw and both eyes open as he watched Joe cook. Occasionally he lapped his long tongue around his gleaming teeth.

The pancakes turned out perfectly and Faraday got the first batch! He sniffed them and whimpered for more syrup—and Joe gave him more. Peggy became indignant. Faraday had already eaten his dog food. She hadn't eaten anything, and it had been her idea to get up! Neither Joe nor Faraday had wanted to get out of bed, and there Faraday was, having an extended breakfast, and she hadn't even had starters. She began to feel hostile.

Faraday hadn't done anything to change Peggy's adamant dislike of dogs, though he was so lazy that she was no longer terrified of him. She could outrun him anytime, he was so slow, so reluctant to even try to move. The only thing on him that got any exercise, besides his mouth chewing food, were his eyes which rolled from side to side, keeping any chance of more food under observation.

Joe absentmindedly handed Peggy a glass of Tang as he turned the eggs and added more batter to the griddle. The morning air was lovely as she sipped her drink, and the aroma of fried bacon seductively lingered to make her hungry stomach growl in anticipation.

Slowly starving to death as she waited, she sat looking west along the electrical line that serviced the shack. Its appearance was in keeping with the shabby house. The line was attached to fence posts, trees, and an occasional, deliberately set pole that was nothing but a crooked, branchless mesquite trunk. Definitely a homemade electrical system. But ragtag as it was, it marched straight west.

"What electrical company supplies the shack? Henry bring it in himself?" Her tone touched on derision.

"He owns the system. It's based at his wells."

How interesting that Henry would have his very own electrical system. She bet it never failed. He would have a couple of hides nailed to the barn if his freezer defrosted. She turned and looked east to see how it was handled on beyond the shack, and it was then she realized that *it stopped at the shack*!

Her mind was working so hard that she almost didn't notice Joe put the plate in front of her. When she did, she immediately dug into the eggs, bacon, and pancakes stacked on it. All the while her mind was figuring that it couldn't be too far to the oil wells if this was Henry's private line. And it went west. All she had to do was follow the line and she would find her way to the offices. She could escape.

Suddenly she stared at the empty plate and was appalled that she had eaten all that food. Her busy brain had not realized what her hand was feeding her mouth, and her mouth had accepted it all, chewed it, and swallowed it, and she was...stuffed!

"What a hungry girl you were! I thought you were simply an early riser. You must have been starved!" Joe smiled at her, that chipped tooth tantalizing her. "Want some more?"

"Uh...no, thank you." As it was she would not be able to get up from the chair. "I don't believe I realized Henry had a large site down there."

"It isn't big at all. Just a few wells. He'd never have a geta-way cabin close to a big operation; they'd never leave him alone." He paused, then tilted his head back and narrowed his eyes at her. "It's an automatic operation. No crew."

"Lots of them run that way. I think the pumpers look like praying mantises."

"Ummm." He wasn't paying much attention.

"Martians stealing the liquid from the earth's ground?"

"Right." He drew the word out in an absentminded way.

She needed to get his mind off the power line. "It'd be nice if there were a couple of flat stones right there where everyone steps off the porch."

"Ummm," he said again, very neutral.

"And a brace would keep the porch corner from sagging farther and straining all those other boards. If it was fixed now, it would last longer."

"Mmmmm." He eyed her suspiciously. "You're not planning on trying to get away from here, are you?"

"Don't be silly. How could I? Where could I go without shoes?"

"If I had to chase you down and retrieve you from quicksand, or rescue you from some...dog pack, I'd handcuff you to me. If you think swimming bare-bottomed in the pond at night with me was shocking, you'd find living handcuffed to me something else entirely."

"You're perfectly awful."

"I'm perfectly awesome?"

"I didn't say awesome, I said awful."

"I'd rather be awesome." He nodded in decision.

He was. Awesome and beautiful, and he had that tooth that made her want to kiss him and let her tongue explore that chip. She blurted in distraction, "How did you learn to scrub clothes so well?" Now where had she found that question?

He did give her an interested look before he replied, "In Canada, the summer after high school." Then he settled a bit and went on, "I was madly in love with a willing girl called Sunny, and she made my dad's hair stand on end and my mother's eyes pop, so somehow I found myself in Canada with nine other males my age and a guide who was fussy as an old...uh...fussbudget, and we had to be neat and orderly and scrub our clothes with a brush on a scrub board. What a drag."

"Where the other nine acquainted with Sunny, also?"

"Or someone like her."

"Then the Canadian trip was a cure-all?"

"At the end of the summer, when I came back, I found that Sunny had to frown and concentrate before she pretended to remember me."

"Aw."

"It was a revealing experience."

"And it turned you off women entirely?"

"Well, I wouldn't say *that*, exactly."

"What did your parents say about Sunny? Did they talk you into giving her up? How did they handle it?"

"We didn't discuss her. They just said as how I'd earned the trip, and they were so excited about me going. They didn't notice I was somewhat lacking in enthusiasm. But my dad did say to me, 'Joseph, this'll make a man of you.'

"My dad always called me Joseph because as a child he'd had a hound named Joe. Mother said dad called me Joseph so he'd remember not to whistle for me, snap his fingers or command me to heel. Dad learned habits so thoroughly he never could give them up. Mother said she was twenty years coaxing him out of the top bunk." He grinned at her, and she got to see the chipped tooth again.

"How did you crack off the corner of your tooth?"

"Well, now, that's a long and terrible story. It isn't safe for me to tell you about it. I can't have you frightened unduly while you're in my care. Henry wouldn't like it."

"I am not Francine." She said it with reasonable calm for a change. "How can I convince you of that? You have rejected my perfectly good driver's license."

He watched her, smiling in a way that could lead an unwary female astray. "Convince me." And his voice made her have to resist flinging herself into his arms.

"I am Margaret Indiana Dillon. My mother is Annabelle Phillips Dillon. My father is Colonel Mathew Treadwell Dillon. I have three brothers, Treadwell, then Phillip and Gary. I am the youngest. We live in San Antonio because my dad retired after thirty years in the army. It's where my mother's people all live. That's the reason dad gives—as if he's indulging her—but actually it's because all his friends married San Antonio girls, and they've all retired there, too. And—"

"Why, that's just amazing! You've done a remarkable job of it. I'll bet you've figured out a whole entire lifetime for me. Do go on."

"All of what I've told you is *true*!" She flung out her arms.

"Francine is from San Antonio and her daddy is also retired from the army."

"But *her* daddy's name is Fullerton! You are the hardest-headed man!"

"No, I'm not either. I'm patient, logical, and lovable."

"Oh, go smoke a cigarette."

"Man, you've got a mean streak in you *that wide*!"

"Come on, get up. I'll do the breakfast dishes while you go down to the creek bed and get some flat stones to put there by the porch."

"You want me to go all the way to the creek on this hot August day and dig out stones?"

"Why not?" she asked heartlessly.

"I'll take the truck." He sighed elaborately.

"It...doesn't...work," she said succinctly and through her teeth.

"It does," he enunciated back. "If you know how." He was so sassy that a woman wanted to go over and...but not Peggy. She knew better.

She wasn't quick enough. He strode over to the truck and opened the hood, and she had only picked her barefooted way there when he slammed it shut. He got in and the motor instantly roared to life. He grinned and said invitingly, "Come on along." Then he opened the door for Faraday.

She would be left there all by herself? "I have to...do the dishes." She lifted her chin then and said more forcefully, "Last night's *and* this morning's."

"We shall return." He gave her a flippant wave of his hand and roared off, moving over the uneven ground carefully, with Faraday sitting beside him.

Peggy was alone. She went into the shack and found the sheet without the top hem. Then she ripped off the bottom hem to hold her suit sleeves on her feet and tried them on to gauge the needed length of the pieces and cut them. There! With opportunity, she was ready.

Why would she leave? That question crowded in. It would be very tempting—for a professional virgin—to stay and learn if she really *was* committed to being one. Joe would supply the solution to that question.

Her decision had been attained from observation and surmise. Actually, a great contributing factor was that she had never really been tempted.

The several men who had been persistent in their pursuit of her had pronounced her cold. One had said "frigid," then turned up his collar and shivered as he told her that he pitied any man who might be trapped into marriage with her, but—he had added—the poor fool could always sleep in the freezer in order to warm up.

What was it about Joe that was different from all the other men she had been introduced to or had dated? He had simply stood next to her in an elevator and she had been attracted in a most scandalous manner. Her body vibrated to his, her fingers twitched to touch him, and she longed to have him close to her.

If she allowed the least little crack in her reserve, she would throw herself into his willing arms and find out if she really was frigid. What a word to use to taunt a woman. A man who would do that was no man at all.

Joe would never say that to a woman. If *she* said she was frigid, he would look surprised, then he would smile and expose his chipped tooth, and he would say, "You trying to fool this Texas boy?" He would say, "Come here, honey," as he tilted his head back, encouraging her closer, and his eyes would close down a bit, and then...and then...

She had better get the washing up done. Joe had put the pan of soaking dishes on the dying fire. He had sprinkled his do-anything soap on top of them, and now they only needed to be rinsed.

He wasn't back yet. It sounded as if he were slinging a sledgehammer against stone down there along the bluff. She stacked the dishes back on the shelves above the freezer, and then was left without anything else to do. She took her purse and fished out her makeup.

Just because one stayed in a shack, one did not have to look as if one belonged there. Satisfied that she was not trying to look good to Joe, she carefully cleaned her face, made up her eyes, ran lip gloss over her mouth, and surveyed herself in the minute mirror.

She took off the bandanna and really brushed her hair with Joe's brush. She leaned over and gave it a hard brushing and then smoothed the silken mane into place. She folded the big bandanna into a long tube and used it to tie her hair back.

In the tiny mirror she gave herself a rather strange, slow smile that startled a part of her awareness. She didn't puzzle over the look; she put away the mirror and went to sit on the porch.

He still wasn't back. If she had known that getting a couple of stones would take so much time, she could already be over the hill and going west along the electrical line. She went inside the shack and found a can of dehydrated lemonade and hunted up a pitcher. She pumped water from the well, made a batch of lemonade, and put it in the refrigerator.

She paced restlessly, then found a hand scythe, nicely coated in oil, that was hanging in the privy. She took the scythe to the front of the shack and cut the weeds around the porch.

She was so engrossed with getting the weeds even that she was surprised when she saw the truck turning to back up to the porch. She stood up to watch and frowned at the tripod rigged on the back of the truck.

Joe climbed down from the cab and stood looking at her, while Faraday slid out beside him. Joe's look activated all her sensual cells and touched her erogenous zones. All that with one look! Peggy knew then that he had never met a frigid woman. Or maybe the sentence should be: no woman, meeting Joe, could be frigid.

He tilted his hat back on his sweaty, dust-streaked forehead, and his eyes examined her efforts at tidiness. "You're ruining this place."

She gasped and looked around at the neat weeds.

"You're making it tidy and pretty. Henry likes things casual. You're going to irritate him, you know. He comes here to 'get back to nature' and not have to *do* anything about the place. See?"

"Well...it's...just..." She gestured indignantly.

"The next thing you know, you'll slap a coat of paint on it and really ruin it."

"It could use some."

"You're a genuine, natural-born nest builder."

"I am not!"

"You'll get married and you'll convince your husband you want ten kids, and the poor guy will do anything you want him to and he'll work his fingers to the very bone so you can live like a queen."

"I'm...frigid."

He laughed immoderately.

He had reacted exactly as she had figured he would, but she felt the need to convince him. She sputtered, "I am, too!"

He dismissed that as worthless and ambled over to the pump. He was tired. She suddenly remembered how hard it had been for him to get out of bed, and she had made him go down and bring back rocks for a step by the porch. "I made some lemonade," she said softly.

"That sounds good. What a thoughtful thing to do."

She said, "Sit there on the porch. I'll get you—" Suddenly she stopped short. How nest builder-ish of her! She stood there with her lips parted, hesitating, but feeling bad because she knew he was hot and tired; and she *had* been the cause of it, wanting that stupid stone. Well, the lemonade was her choice! Firmly she went into the shack and poured two glasses and took them out to him.

"Thanks, honey. That's going to really hit the spot."

She was pleased.

"Could Faraday have a little?" Joe asked. "He's exhausted." The dog rolled his eyes pitifully.

"What did he do?" she asked scornfully. "He never does anything."

"He had to sit there and watch me work," Joe replied, as if that made it obvious.

She laughed as she went over and poured some lemonade into Faraday's bowl. He waited, but she returned to sit at the table on the porch. Finally Faraday groaned, heaved himself up and shuffled over and lapped the lemonade. After two laps he turned a baleful eye on Peggy.

"It probably doesn't have enough sugar for him," Joe explained. "But I think it's just perfect." He gave her an extremely nice smile, but he didn't expose his chipped tooth.

Joe had to dig away some of the hard surrounding earth by the porch because his flat rock was too big for the indentation that people's feet had made. Peggy thought the rock was perfect, and she exclaimed enthusiastically, "It's enormous! We could have a trail of stepping-stones right over to the fence."

That caused him to stop digging in order to look at her as if she had turned a lilac color to blend with her purple suit. "Path?"

"Just to the fence?" She smiled.

"Honey, that fence is just about as nonexistent as any fence can be. With so few cedar posts still left, it really isn't a 'fence' at all."

"It could be fixed."

"Why?"

"To...keep the local sheep out?"

"The sheep are the lawn mowers. With the grass and weeds short, it's too hot for the snakes and it keeps them away."

"There are mechanical lawn mowers." She dismissed sheep as she looked around. "A garden would be nice...over there."

His smile was very tender. "Nest builder."

"I am not!" she said huffily. "Wanting things nice doesn't mean a woman wants to...to build a *nest*! It's just having things neat."

"Ummm." He tilted his hat down and picked up his refilled glass of lemonade, but he had a smile on his lips as he sipped some more of the ice cold drink. Then he leaned on his shovel as he said very kindly, "There's nothing wrong with nest builders. Where would we all be if there weren't men and women who had the instinct to build a nest to hold their children?" He gave her a level look from under his hat brim. "My best friends all want nests for the women they love, who want to care for them and their children. It's natural, and the men I want around me are the nurturing kind who care what happens to other people, too."

"Yes." She could understand that, but she blushed for some strange reason.

"You move so nicely. You move different from a man."

"I'm built differently. My hips..."

"Ummmmmmm." It was a sound rather than a comment.

She assumed a lecturing attitude. "Men's knees go out when they walk. Their torsos stay firm and their knees go out. Women are built wider and it's their hips that shift...." She stumbled to a halt.

"You move your arms so prettily." He leaned his chin on his gloved hands at the top of the long handled spade and looked at her. "When you turn your head, your neck is so graceful and your shoulders are so feminine."

She snorted in an unfeminine way and scolded, "Quit your loafing and get back to work!"

And he laughed.

Because Peggy had gotten them all up at the crack of dawn, the stone was settled into its new home just before lunch. He used the block and tackle supported by the tripod on the back of the truck and efficiently lowered the stone into place.

Joe had sent her up to the mill to bathe in the sun-warmed barrel; and as she fixed their lunch he went up to bathe in her left-over water. She found the thought of that rather unsettling.

He said his muscles were too tired for him to swim in the pond, they would cramp in the cold water, and he didn't mind sharing anything with her. That shot a thrill through her stomach that about paralyzed her, because the thing she was thinking of sharing wasn't bath water.

She mixed the tuna with reconstituted celery and onion, then added mayonnaise and some pickle relish. She made him two sandwiches and then two more, and she watched wide-eyed as he ate them all, plus two glasses of reconstituted milk and two pieces of yesterday's pie.

She kept walking off the porch and stepping on the stone as she returned; she had to try the wide flat stone several times. She was extremely pleased with it and commented on how clever he was. "It's just so nice. It looks as if the house is deliberate. You know? That it was meant to be here and not just dropped down out of the sky." But then she went over and tested the sagging corner of the porch.

Joe watched her as he chewed; a smile played around his mouth, and his eyes were amused. He had on a white dress shirt that he had gleaned from the stack of clean clothes, and he wore some shorts that were very soft and skimpy. His legs were strong, hairy, brown, and muscular, and his form thrilled her body.

She kept sneaking glances at him, and she initiated a conversation so that she had excuses to watch him. Her conduct made her blush, but she couldn't help herself. She did resist touching him.

She had concentrated so hard on keeping him busy that she was worn out herself. Without consulting her, he carried the mattress up to its place under the oak, and she knew how tired he was and tried to help him carry it.

He laid it down, and she put both pillows on it. She said, "No, don't go for the quilt. I trust you. We'll share." She raised bleak eyes to him, because she had tricked him and when he was asleep, she would sneak away and flee, and she might hurt his feelings.

She put a hand to her forehead at the thought of hurting his feelings—and why should that bother her, she wondered—and dropped down onto the edge of the mattress. She pretended to close her eyes and fall asleep so that he would sleep, too, and she could leave.

She dreamed that she finally had her fingers in his silken hair. How had she gotten his hat off? His hand was on her breast, kneading it in a lovely way. She was being kissed, and deep in her throat she was making an extremely wanton sound as her body strained against him. She became conscious—and all of it was true!

That was exactly what was happening, and she loved it!

She was so startled that she didn't move and just pretended to be asleep for a little while longer. No harm in that. She was being taken advantage of while she slept. She couldn't help what happened if she was asleep.

She allowed him his way, and he was furtive and delicious. How shocking! How mind-bendingly, dis*grace*fully, appallingly marvelous!

She couldn't respond too much. He might suspect that she was awake, so she stayed limp and tried not to react. But he did. He touched and teased and petted and kissed and nudged and was plainly outrageous. And she relished every tantalizing nuance.

His breath was hot and came in short blasts, his hands were scalding on her cool flesh, and his kisses were molten. How lovely! She couldn't stop herself from twisting slightly, and she swallowed noisily. She was almost panting.

It was his hand sliding up the inside of her thigh that forced her to "wake up." If his hard hand reached her soft core, he would know she was shamming. So she stiff-armed him with betrayingly reluctant arms and gasped, "Why, Joe! What are you doing?" She did a lousy job of it.

"Shhhh." His eyes were laughing. "Don't scream. You'll upset Faraday."

She had to swallow before she could look down her body to his fingers moving so marvelously on her bare breast, and she had to blink several times before she could look back into his eyes, prevent an answering smile, and with assumed indignation demand again, "What are you doing?"

He replied logically in a low rumble, "Not smoking." His eyes dropped down to her naked chest. "I have to do something with my hands." He had to bite his lower lip to minimize his grin.

"You have to stop this!" Her voice wavered instead of being hostile and firm, and her own hands continued sliding through his hair.

He trailed kisses along her jaw, and his errant hand left her breast to slide down around her back and pull her tightly against him so he could hug her close. It was so nice, and the thrills she felt were enhanced by the sound of pleasure rumbling in his chest.

He continued to stroke her and kiss her and move his face on hers, but he did not get *on* with it. Finally she asked in a breathy voice, "Are...you...going to ravish me?" She frowned over the sound of it. It had not come out just exactly as one would hope such a question would sound when spoken by a professional virgin.

The pupils of his eyes were enormous. And since he was so occupied with her body, he was very close and his sweet breath was quick and hot on her face as his head came back to hers, and he kissed her in a talented, squishy way.

While she did not actually kiss him back, she waited for the opportunity and licked her tongue along that chipped tooth, and he groaned as if he had strained a muscle.

She knew he had worked very hard that morning. "Where does it hurt?" she asked softly, and her fingers left his hair and gently prodded the muscles of his shoulders.

"Not there."

She assumed his unsteady voice was from pain. She shouldn't have worked him so hard that morning with the stepping-stone. She had been unkind. He was very brave. He must hurt so badly to groan that way, and yet he was using those muscles to hold her so nicely. "Are you...going to ravish me?"

That sounded almost hopeful! She sucked in a breath, but couldn't think of anything else she wanted to know or to tell him. Was he or wasn't he?

"How could I ravish a virgin?"

That made her sincerely, honestly, full-out indignant. "What do you mean?" she huffed and puffed. "How did you know? How could you possibly...?"

He leaned on his elbows and grinned down at her. "Anyone seeing you in that sheet, with your arm clamped over your pretty breasts and your knees locked together that way, would suspect."

"Well, I've never...it's just that...you see...I'm frigid."

"Oh, yes." But he didn't sound sincere. He nuzzled her ear and along the side of her throat and blew his breath there and rubbed his day's whiskers gently along the tender flesh on her collarbone and in slow swirls down around her breast.

She sucked in her breath and put her head back as her knees came up and her back arched. All frigid women probably did that. It wasn't any indication that she was wanton or agreeable or inviting. "Are you...?" She couldn't seem to keep herself from reminding him. But she just wanted to know if he was going to ravish her so she could close her eyes and...brace herself.

When he kissed her again, her tongue sneaked another touch to that tooth.

"Some day I'll tell you how that tooth happened." He appeared to believe they would be seeing each other for some time.

Cautiously she said, "I know what happened. You forced a woman and she bit it off."

He laughed, leaning his face down on her chest, and his hot breath against her cool skin caused all sorts of distractions all through her body and down past her knees to her toes, making them spread voluptuously.

"I suppose you dragged her off to one or another of Henry's hideaways and had your way with her? Was it here?" Why did she keep harping on seduction?

"You're the first woman I've ever stolen."

"You know you can't just take the law into your own hands."

"It's not the law my hands want to hold." And he moved them to indicate what he had in mind.

That left her speechless. When she could manage to speak, she blurted, "What would Henry think if he drove up and saw us here on the mattress?"

"So." He looked down at her. "You admit you're Francine?"

"No!"

"Then why do you keep shoving old Henry up my nose?"

"Well..." She didn't know if she should point out the fact that they were out there all alone.

"Just because we're out here all alone?" Joe asked, as if he'd read her mind. "Do you think the threat of some other man will slow me down?" He leaned and brushed his lips across hers, and she was surprised to feel the distant reactions that ran clear from her lips all the way down her body. "Do you feel threatened?" Joe asked in a remarkably unanswerable way. "I told you I'd take care of you."

"You promised that no harm would come to me, on your honor."

"Oh, did that include making love? What harm is there in that?"

She couldn't think of any.

"As I recall, I said at the shack—"

"Cabin."

"Cabin?" He looked over his shoulder at it. "It's a shack."

"I know that now, but at the time you said 'cabin,' and I assumed it would be a normal Henry-accommodation with a pool and air-conditioning, and everything would be reasonable."

"Surprised you, didn't I?"

"Somewhat."

"Are you trying to distract me from what I was up to?"

"Ummmmhuummm," she lied, and her eyes were full of regret.

He smoothed back her tousled hair and kissed her forehead. "I suppose you're reasonably safe." He moved far enough from her so that she could sit up.

He was letting her go? That annoyed her. She sat up reluctantly and fumbled with the buttons on her suit jacket.

"Take it off." The suggestion was made to sound off-hand. "Go around topless; I won't try to ravish you. I may consider it, if you smile or lift your arms or flip back your hair...it's so soft and pretty. Did I tell you that?"

And, silly woman that she was, she actually considered just taking off the jacket and doing all those things.

Six

The afternoon was gone. Despite all her firm resolve, Peggy had both fallen asleep for real and slept longer than Joe. She had ruined that day's chance to escape. She stood up finally, leaned over, and picked up the pillows.

He patted her bottom, and she jerked around. Why did she feel so peevish toward him? He hadn't ravished her.

She gave him a cool look and stomped off toward the shack with as firm a stride as one could manage barefooted. And her temper did not improve. In fact, it worsened when she discovered Joe watching her with hot eyes that brimmed with teasing humor. What was so blasted funny?

She shot him a killing glance and thought she would like to see his face the next day—after he found out she had escaped.

When he found her gone and realized he had missed the chance to... Well, that didn't matter. She would get away. She slammed the dishes on the table and sulked all through supper.

Joe cooked the meal. He had retrieved his dried denims from the brace of the windmill and pulled them on. And he wore his hat and boots, and was again bare-chested until it was time to eat.

He thawed a carton of chili that was Henry's concoction which he'd entered in the Great Texas Chili Cook-Off. Joe explained that Henry's entry hadn't won because no one could eat it without scalding his stomach.

By chance they had discovered that though it couldn't be eaten full strength, cutting it to one-fourth chili to two cans of pinto beans and a pile of rice did dilute it enough to be edible. It still made Peggy's eyes water, and it even made Faraday belch.

"I really don't think you ought to give that dog chili." It was the first time she had spoken to Joe since she left the mattress under the oak after he hadn't ravished her.

He gave a very poorly done start of surprise and said, "Well, hello, honey. Where'd you come from?"

"Don't be cute."

"Hot dang! So you think I'm cute?"

"Good grief."

"That guy who said you were cold, did you actually kiss him?" He tilted his head to watch her.

"It's none of your business."

Joe moved impatiently. "I'm so curious, I'm about to die. Did *he* kiss *you*?"

She tried to think of something shattering to say to him, but ended up blurting, "Yes!" in irritation as she flared her eyes at him.

"I've got to meet that poor fool." He shook his head, resettled his Stetson, and leaned back to contemplate the sky. Then he straightened up and said, "It could be this pure, country-fresh Texas air that set you off."

"Set me...off?"

"Made you all hot and willing."

"I was not!" she sputtered.

He laughed.

Extra FREE BONUS!

When you return the postpaid order card with the bouquet attached, you'll also receive a FREE Mystery Gift. Send for yours today!

SILHOUETTE DESIRE® Silhouette Books,
120 Brighton Rd., P.O. Box 5084, Clifton, NJ 07015-9956

Place the bouquet here

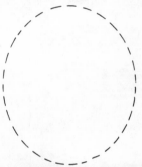

Then take 4 FREE books and your Mystery Gift.

Yes, please send me the 4 newest Silhouette Desire novels FREE and without obligation, along with my Mystery Gift. Unless you hear from me after I receive them, send me 6 new Silhouette Desire novels for a FREE 15-day examination each month as soon as they are published. I understand that you will bill me a total of just $11.70 (a $13.50 value), with no additional charges of any kind. There is no minimum number of books that I must buy and I can cancel at any time. The first 4 books and Mystery Gift are mine to keep.

NAME _____ (please print)

ADDRESS _____

CITY/STATE _____ ZIP _____

Terms and prices subject to change. Your enrollment is subject to acceptance by Silhouette Books.

SILHOUETTE DESIRE is a service mark and registered trademark. CAD625

Take 4 FREE BOOKS

Plus a FREE Mystery Gift...

See the details inside on how you can get 4 FREE Silhouette Desire novels and a Mystery Gift *with no obligation!*

That pretty much finished that conversation. She finished eating and sat there, moving around restlessly in her chair; then she got up and slammed things around as she tidied up.

"Just soak them," he advised. "Put them in the pan and I'll put the pan on the coals and by morning it'll be—"

"A mess."

"Naw. Nothing like that. It'll be easy."

Easy? The way he thought she was? Wouldn't the other men who had tried with her all be astonished to learn Joseph Richards thought she was hot and willing?

They not only wouldn't believe it, they would fall to the floor in helpless hilarity. How she would love to see that.

She paced around the "yard," that area in front of the shack; then she stomped off to the pond and walked around the edge—looking for alligator slides. She was positive there weren't any. Almost positive.

Joe had ambled along after her and watched her, his thumbs hooked into his jean pockets, his fingers spread on his hips. He moved so well. He looked around, he watched her, he kept track of the area, and he followed her. "Find any?" he inquired pleasantly.

Knowing exactly what he meant, and annoyed by that, she replied, "Any what?"

"Alligators."

"I'm not that naïve."

"I knew you'd know I was funning you. Even though you're a city girl and a world traveler, I knew you'd recognize that I wouldn't let you swim where there was any danger."

How clever of him to reassure her and yet allow her to pretend she really hadn't believed him all along. He was kind.

"With your hair loose like that, you look like a cover for a book that everyone would just have to buy."

He was smooth-tongued, too.

"I thought you agreed to go around topless," he complained. "Why don't you take off that hot old jacket? I promise—almost certainly—I wouldn't touch you. It is possible I'd sneak a look or two, but I would certainly try not to touch you."

"Since I'm so hot and willing, how do you know I wouldn't attack you?" For a hot and willing woman, her tone was quite parsimonious.

"Okay." He held out his arms. "Attack."

"Men!" She flung out her own arms, then lifted her chin—and her chest—and automatically turned southeast toward the Gulf breeze. She wasn't posing, of course; she was simply enjoying the soft wind. But there was no wind. It was hot, humid and still. There was an odd restlessness in the quiet stillness.

"I'm going swimming," she declared bravely.

"Wait...twenty more minutes."

"An hour after eating? That's been proved silly," she scoffed. "It doesn't matter if you swim right after eating."

"Well, I'm just an old-fashioned boy, and since I'm responsible for you, I'd prefer you to wait. I'd sure as hell die if anything happened to you. That pond's deep."

He was too earnest for her to defy him. So she strolled with elaborate indifference around the end of the pond, thereby proving that she was delaying on her own behalf, not his. He trailed casually along after her. Faraday watched from the shade of the shack.

Another night was approaching. Peggy would have been with him for two days and two nights when she left tomorrow. It seemed they had always been together. What would she get him to do tomorrow that would exhaust him while she stayed rested? He had to nap the next afternoon while she made her escape.

If she didn't get away, how long would he keep her there? Why hadn't the roadblockers been back to check on her? What sort of men were they that they would allow one man to carry off a strange woman and keep her in the wilderness?

What about Francine? It had been Francine who had gotten her into this mess. Why wasn't Francine here, rescuing her? What sort of "twin" would allow her to be left all alone in a one-room shack with this mind-blowing man? A man who didn't keep a decent distance, but who tempted her until she was mindless.

And Henry! He had been informed that she was here. Where the blue blazes was Henry? He had to know that Francine wasn't here...or had Francine disappeared, too? Perhaps Henry knew she wasn't Francine, but he was searching for Francine somewhere else and had just forgotten Peggy?

How had she ever been talked into this impossible situation? What was she to do? Go to Joe and put her arms around him and rub her hungry body against his marvelously masculine physique and just indulge her curiosity? What would it be like to make love to that tempting man? Why was she so curious to do that now with him when she had never been interested with any other man?

There was an excellent possibility that she just might not be frigid. She would very much like to take his clothes off and simply explore him. Touch him. Look at him. She would like to run her fingers over him and see what would happen. What would it be like to make love with Joe? She strongly suspected that it might not be too bad.

Although the wind had died, there were clouds building in the west. She turned and looked from them back to Joe, who was still following along after her, and he smiled at her in the dimming light.

He really disturbed her equilibrium. She had to swallow, lick her lips, and clear her throat before she asked, "Are the twenty minutes up?" And with the question, she betrayed the fact that she was obeying him.

He turned his watch up and replied, "By the time you take off all your clothes, wash them out in the barrel there, and hang them up on the braces, it'll be dark and you can swim unseen. I'll get you a clean, dry shirt." He strode off toward the shack.

Peggy figured that by the time he reached the shack, got the shirt and started back, she could be in the water. She glanced back; he was already halfway there.

She peeled off the jacket, the skirt, and her underwear, took the bucket from the nail and dipped out enough water to wash the clothes and did that quickly. Then she wrung them out, hung them up, and turned back for a quick look at the shack— but ten feet away, there stood Joe! His hands were on his hips, his legs braced apart, his hat on the back of his head, and he watched her with a very serious expression on his face.

She folded into herself like the painting *September Morn* and gasped. ''The shirt?''

His hands came up and he fumbled with the buttons on his own shirt as he said, ''Right here.''

''I thought you were going to the shack!''

Then he grinned widely, heartlessly exposing his chipped tooth, and replied, ''I knew you would.''

''Why...Joe!'' But she could finally move, and she stepped down on the wooden bench and dived into the pond...alligators and all. When she came up and looked back, he had shucked off both boots, discarded his pants, and dived from the bank into the pond in the rapidly fading light.

She thrashed off to the other end. She felt both the residual foolish fear of alligators, and real excitement at the naked man who followed her.

If it hadn't been so deeply muddy at the other end, and if the bank hadn't been so steep she couldn't get out without a long, *revealing* struggle, she might have made it out of there. But it *was* muddy, and the bank *was* steep, so she turned to face her fate. There he was. He was naked, she was naked, it was Kismet.

He swam up to the sacrificial maiden, stopped, and treaded water as he grinned. ''Don't panic. The water's so cold I'm completely de-sexed.''

Well, damn! She clenched her teeth in disgust.

They swam beside each other. ''If you get tired,'' he told her, ''you can turn over and float on your back.''

She gave him a cautious look. He was teasing her. If she turned over on her back he would be able to see her. He already had.

"It's cold in this pond," he complained. "If you would put your arms around me, cuddle me close to you, and kiss me a little, I might warm up some and you'd keep me from freezing. It would be the humanitarian thing to do."

Maybe the water hadn't de-sexed him after all. "Keep your distance." But she had been so quick with the words, just to show him she wasn't easy, that she gulped a mouthful of that alligator water and, as she had once before, she choked.

Naturally he was chivalrous. He lifted her and patted her back, but he lifted her over his shoulder and held her close to him—and he laughed. When she finished coughing and struggled to be free, he slid her down him.

Her body couldn't have felt like anything nice to his. Her flesh was cold and wet. She must have felt like a dead fish. She glanced at him, and his face was serious.

Then the day was gone, and it was pitch dark again. It scared her for a minute until her eyes could adjust to the change. "Where's the bench?"

"This way." He took her hand and towed her to the bench. When she reached to lift herself out of the water, his hands went down her body in a lingering caress, and then he put his hand on her bottom and boosted her out.

She considered running, but that would be futile. How could she see? And she remembered how effortlessly he had caught her when she had tried to escape down the track. It would be a worthless gesture to run. She was enflamingly naked, and he was so nakedly male...there was simply no help for her. She could only be brave about it.

He wasn't at all shy. He came out of the water. He knew she was looking at him over her shoulder, and that she could see him, but he didn't turn away or cross his hands in front of himself or anything. Instead he ran his hands over his hair and shook it to get the water out. Then his hands stripped the water from his arms and chest as he watched her.

He moved with a slow, male walk toward her as he wiped the excess water from his body and flipped it from his hands.

Turned modestly away from him, she just stood there and dripped.

He reached toward her, and she closed her eyes, her head tilted back as she took a deep bracing breath—and he reached beyond her for the still damp but already drying jacket.

He used it to dry her. He did it quickly, briskly. He didn't do it slowly or sensuously, but efficiently. After he finished her hair, he handed her his shirt, then dried himself before he shook out her jacket and replaced it on the mill's brace.

Surely he wouldn't ravish her right there on the concrete base of the windmill? It would be a little wild, and something she would remember as rather primitive and unusual—to lose her virginity in such a place—but the concrete would be abrasive on her back.

He took the shirt from her hands, and her skin got excited, her insides prickled, and she grew a bit dizzy. She had heard that virgins never liked it the first time.

He held the shirt for her, and she gradually realized that he meant for her to put it on. He probably intended to go back to the shack to the bed. She put her arms into the sleeves and turned toward him as he took up his trousers and carelessly slid his muscular legs into them and zipped them up. Then he pulled on his boots.

With three older brothers who were very close to her in age, the male body was no secret wonder. Why was Joe's? Why were her eyes drawn to him? Why did her fingers itch to be on him? It was very strange. Especially so since she hadn't eaten any lime Popsicles all day, and at twenty-two she had a long way to go before she reached thirty-five and the peak of female sexual hunger.

As he had the night before, he easily lifted her in his arms and carried her back to the shack. She sat quite properly. She didn't curl against his strong hairy chest, or tuck her face into the hollow between his jaw and shoulder.

She did put her arm across his back, but only to help him with her weight. He didn't appear to need any help, though; he carried her effortlessly.

She knew what the Sabine women in ancient Italy had felt like after they were stolen away, carried off by the men of Rome who wanted wives. The women must have felt just this way, each one helpless, a little scared, knowing what was coming...intrigued by a marvelously good-looking, charming, humorous, strong man with a chipped tooth. Then she realized that the abductors of the Sabine women couldn't all have had chipped teeth.

Again she asked, "How did you chip your tooth?" Her breath was a little thin and gaspy—probably because of the uneven ground.

He turned his head down to hers, and with her mouth so handy, he kissed her. He stopped walking and kissed her longer. Her head went back on his shoulder, and she crossed her ankles and swung her feet a little, and although her right hand floated around in the air in an aimless way, she didn't put it alongside his jaw or run her fingers into his hair. She knew enough not to encourage him.

When he lifted his mouth minimally, she said in a faint unsure voice, "You're not to get into my bed."

He didn't move his mouth any farther away as he replied in a sure, low voice, "'Course not. Now that I know you don't want me to, I won't."

"I mean it." She breathed the three words.

"Don't worry about it, honey. I'm an honorable man."

"You kidnapped—"

"Other than that."

And by golly, he set her on her feet on the porch, kissed her good night, and went off!

She stood there a while, but the mosquitoes were hungry in the still muggy night, so she went inside, climbed into bed, and frowned up toward where the ceiling was in darkness. He was out there with all those mosquitoes and no shirt.

She got out of bed, felt through the stack of clean clothes folded on the table, found a shirt, changed into it, took his shirt and the repellent and went outside. He was nowhere around.

She went over to the truck, opened the door, and yelped as right next to her a voice growled in warning, "It won't start."

"Where did you come from?" she snapped. "I didn't see you!"

"Are you trying to run away again?"

"Of course not!" she said in a temper. "I was bringing you your shirt and the bug spray."

"You worried about me?"

"Common courtesy." She was aloof.

"You're a darling."

"The mosquitoes are terrible tonight," she explained.

"Wind's dead," he told her. "A storm's coming."

"Oh." She couldn't see his face. She battled with her conscience over her virtue, and compassion won. "I suppose you ought to sleep inside the shack?"

"Why, sure!"

"But not on the bed." She was adamant.

"No." Why should his voice sound so amused? "On the floor with Faraday."

"That dog does not come inside the shack."

"If it storms and he's outside, he'll howl. He...responds to lightning."

"It will...lightning?"

"Brilliantly. It promises to be a wild one."

"How do you know that?"

"Truck radio."

"Oh."

They could hear the wind coming from far, far away. She put a hand on his arm and turned her head in that direction. It was such a long way off, but it roared along the ground, tossing trees and grasses, and the sound mounted as it came closer.

Even knowing what it was, she was frightened, because it was approaching so fast, so relentlessly, and there was nothing that could stop it.

"It's coming." His smile glinted in the dark.

"Yes." Her fingers clutched his arm. Her nerves were strung taut by the sound, and she was tense and spooked.

"Run! Get the north and west windows closed. At the very least that wind will be dusty. I'll close up the truck." He turned away and shouted the last. "Let Faraday inside."

Faraday was wobbling past her, heading for the shack, and even though she ran, as directed, the dog somehow beat her to the porch. The tension mounted as the muttering roar came toward them. It sounded like a mob out of control. She slammed down the two windows and hoped the roof didn't leak. She moved to the door, looking for Joe, and stumbled over the dog, who had flopped on the one open space on the floor.

Then she remembered that her clothes were on the mill brace! She burst from the shack and started to run there, but met Joe on the way. He yelled above the nearing roar, "Get back to the shack!"

"My suit!" She flung a dramatic arm toward the windmill. "I'll get it!"

"And my...*panties*!" she hollered.

"Right." He disappeared, but his voice came back. "Get inside!"

Above her the oak stirred restlessly. It was as if her tension had communicated itself to the tree. The limbs moved, and the leaves whispered, as if they were nervous. Where was Joe? The roar mounted. It seemed hard for her to breathe, and her heart pounded. The storm was going to be a bad one.

Where was Joe? "Joe!" she called. The windmill wasn't that far away. Had he fallen into the pond? With it so dark and the stars gone, he could have lost his sense of direction and fallen into the water, where his boots would pull him down. She started to the rescue.

The wind hit her hard, sending her staggering back. The oak swung creaking limbs as if resisting, fighting back against the overwhelming wind. The roar was frightening. Dust, sticks, leaves and debris were hurtled along, and her skin was prickled as her hair streamed away from her face.

She screamed into it. "*Joe*!" Her shirt was plastered to her as her body was chilled by the summer norther.

In her mind she could see the windmill topple over, knocking Joe to the ground, pinning him there. "Joe!" she screamed. And hands reached from *behind*, grabbing her, stopping her. She shrieked like the heroine of a horror movie as she turned, beating with her fists, straining to get loose and go help Joe.

"Hey!" he said. "*Peggy*! It's okay. It's me."

She stopped. "Joe?" The lightning illuminated his chipped tooth. "Joe!" She flung her arms around his neck and knocked him a step backward. His arms closed around her, and he laughed.

"A wild woman in a wild storm!" His voice was a growl in her ear, and the sound of his throaty laugh was wicked, though it was almost torn away by the storm.

The lightning flashed and crackled, hissing and alive. The thunder rumbled in the ground under their feet, and Joe hurried her to the shack. "Hustle up, woman; I don't want to lose you."

It was as if he magically transported them inside the shack, where Faraday was lying under the bed and howling. The lightning zapped outside; the thunder shook the ground and rattled the house and everything in it—including Peggy's teeth. If the dog hadn't been under the bed, Peggy would have crawled right in herself.

Joe retrieved the chairs the wind had flung into the yard and brought them inside. Peggy sat on one, then put her head on the table and her arms over her head. Joe pulled his chair up close to her and put one hand on the nape of her neck. "Fearless Francine? The defiant damsel afraid of a little old summer storm?" The teasing in his voice was unforgivable.

The rain hit in buckets. The entire storm was concentrated over that one miserable shack in which were one hyper woman, a howling dog, and an amused man.

He pulled her onto his lap, saying, "With just a little cooperation I could distract you very nicely. When you can't control circumstances, distraction is the solution."

But she only wrapped her arms around his head and tucked her own head along his throat and shivered.

"The way I have it figured is that you have a hell of a guilty conscience about something, and you think this storm is retribution. So I say to myself, what could possibly be troubling this young innocent-seeming woman? And the answer came to me—just like that!" He snapped his fingers, making a tiny pop in the maelstrom. "You feel guilty for not letting me make love to you. Right?"

He pulled back, trying to see her face in the lightning flashes, but she just burrowed closer. From under the bed, Faraday whimpered and howled. Joe laughed, and his laugh was genuinely amused.

"This is the perfect time to tell you about how I chipped my front tooth, but such a revelation, in such circumstances, might well tip you over the edge into madness. I can't tell you and risk such consequences. No, I'll tell you the story of my life, carefully editing out the Tale of the Chipped Tooth for a more placid time when you can handle it emotionally."

He shifted his legs and rearranged her a little before he continued. "My life up until lately has been so deadly dull that, listening to it, you'll sleep through the rest of the storm. You might flicker an eyelid now and again during the greater crashes of thunder, but you'll be sedated into euphoric peace."

He never did tell her the actual story of his life; he just droned on about how much it would bore her, and he was so inventive and so funny that she relaxed a little and lay against him, her face hidden in his strong throat as she listened, and she even smiled.

When the storm moved on past and the sound of it became only rumbles in the east, he reached over and flipped back the quilt; then he lifted her and laid her on the bed. She was exhausted and turned immediately over on her side and went to sleep, contemplating a wisp of vagrant thought: Joe had called her Peggy. Out there with the storm boiling around them, he hadn't called her Francine—he had called her Peggy.

Peggy's first thought when she awakened was how lovely it was to have her body so toasty-warm, when the air had been

made so blessedly cool by the freaky August norther. She tried
to stretch out her legs, but ran into a resistant bulk. She opened
her eyes and frowned into Joe's, which were right there, not a
foot away. He was studying her with his usual amused
fascination.

"What are doing on the bed?"

"I did try to stay on the floor," he lied with reassuring ear-
nestness. "But the termites were drowned out by the down-
pour and came through the floor and looked on Faraday and
me as islands in the storm." He licked his lips. "They tickle.
And although I did try to endure them, if I don't get my proper
rest I'm so cross and grouchy—what with quitting smoking and
all—"

"There aren't any termites?"

"Pre-flight mosquitoes?"

She shook her head.

"We were cold and damp down there, honey, and you
weren't using the *entire* bed, so we thought you wouldn't mind
if we—"

"We?" She raised her head and saw that the resistant bulk
taking up the bottom half of her half of the bed was Faraday.
"How did that blob get up on the bed?"

"Well, I did help. Getting him up on the bed is a little like
getting out of the pond." He slid a salacious glance her way.
"There's just times when a body needs a little help from a
friend."

"That dog is not going to sleep on this bed." Indignantly she
pushed her feet down to dislodge him, but the dog growled at
her, yawned, stretched and resettled himself. She didn't mention anything about Joe not being in her bed, and his eyes
sparkled with that knowledge.

Joe said soothingly, "He'll get hungry pretty soon and he'll
get up."

"And what gets you up?" she demanded.

He coughed for a little while; then he said in an unsteady
voice, "You could try." After that he laughed.

Her mind was blank for whole seconds, trying to figure out what he could find so funny about getting out of bed. She ran a hand over her face and hair; then she blushed and sputtered—and pushed.

He really wasn't very push-able. He grinned and said, "Why don't you give me a sweet good morning kiss and we can see if that'll work?"

She did hesitate. It would be lovely to lie in that squeaky bed under the covers, against that warm man on that cool morning, and kiss. But mother always said a girl must not. Peggy had already stepped across all the boundaries and was going full tilt toward helping with her own seduction.

It was past time to straighten up and behave herself. That was hard enough, but making him behave too was about impossible. He enjoyed it all so much.

"Do you really believe I'm Francine?"

"Hummm?"

"That I'm Francine and engaged to your best friend?"

"Well..."

"Am I?"

"Now, honey..."

"Then I'm out of bounds to you."

"Uh..."

"Right?"

And he laughed.

It rained all that day, and it was very cool. She wore an eccentric collection from the clothes pile, but her feet were cold. No socks. At the back, on top of the cupboard, Joe had found a beautiful pair of Henry's hand-made moccasins. He measured carefully, cut them down to her size and restitched them crudely. It took all morning, and they talked about everything under the sun. Joe told her once, "The rodeo circuit's probably the stupidest thing I've ever been involved in."

She could sympathize with stupid. "The stupidest thing I've been involved in is...something like a marriage market."

"Yeah? How's that?"

She hesitated, because if she said she had a fortune to this simple cowboy, it would seem like bragging. It could make him feel...like a lesser man. She chose her words carefully. "My family has been around for a while here in Texas. We used to know everybody. But eventually, with distance and distractions, there are people who don't know one another.

"There's a Men's Club in Dallas that tries to act as matchmakers. It's silly now. There was a time when it was needed, back when travel was difficult, and marriageable daughters were very sheltered, when people were spread out all over the state.

"There was a time when it was needed to get people together. I suppose it's still important if someone is interested. I'm not."

"They've tried to match you up with a waiting line of men?"

"Actually, no. Just one."

"Henry?"

"Not Henry. But a friend of his. Do you know any of the Mulhollands?"

"Mulholland? The name does ring a bell. They matched you up with him?"

"Very stupidly. I declined."

"Poor Mulholland."

"*His* first name is Joe, too."

"There are probably several men named Joe in Texas," Joe said blandly.

"Yes." And that was all he said.

When the shoes were done she was ecstatic. She put them on and walked around and laughed. She gave him a smacking, enthusiastic kiss and told him he was perfectly brilliant.

"You're pleased?"

"I've been barefooted for three days!"

"If I make you something else, will I get another kiss?"

"I don't *need* anything else! After this I'm going to carry a change of underwear, a toothbrush, and moccasins in my purse. Then if some other nut captures me and carries me off, I'll be more comfortable!"

She whooped and flung out her arms. She went out on the porch and looked around the drippy day and smiled at it, then turned back and ran into Joe's chest. Bracing her hands against him, she looked up and exclaimed, "Let's go for a *walk*!"

He was cautious. "Faraday has to eat lunch. And me."

She laughed exuberantly. "He's going to eat lunch *and* you?"

"I believe I've done something exceedingly rash."

"What?"

"I've put you in shoes. The first law of husbands and men who take captives is: keep them barefooted! There's an additional rule that runs right alongside that one." He was studying her soberly.

But she was full of the prospect of walking on the ground without having to pick her way along. She was *free*! Well, almost free.

Seven

Peggy sang as she fixed their lunches and, still keeping her distance, she talked baby-talk to Faraday. The more cheerful she became, the more sober and watchful Joe was, while Faraday rolled a careful eye and kept her in sight.

As they sat at the table, munching on lunch, she said, "Dogs aren't supposed to eat three meals a day."

"Now, how could we possibly sit here, eating, and make Faraday just watch?"

"You're as undisciplined as he is."

"I have a tender heart. I'm not hard-hearted and selfish like some women in this room."

"And you're not truthful."

He expressed great astonishment in the word. "Oh?"

"You said Faraday would howl if he couldn't be inside when it stormed. He *was* inside, and he still howled. He's a coward. I just wonder why anyone pays him stud fees. Think what fat, lazy, cowardly offspring come from him."

"He wasn't afraid of the storm," Joe explained. "He howled to challenge it."

"From under the bed?"

"He was being courteous. The shack is small, and he didn't want to intrude on our floor space."

"Ahhhh."

"I'm happy we cleared that up. I'd hate for you to be misled." He took a bite, chewed, and his eyes met hers. "Speaking of being afraid, weren't you the woman on my lap last night? With her arms choking the very breath from me? And her head hidden in my neck?"

She tidily wiped the edges of her mouth with the corner of a paper towel. "I have learned, in my psych classes, that one way to draw bravery from others is to allow them the feeling of being protective and in control."

"Um-hum, so you just pretended to be afraid so I'd be brave about the storm."

"Of course. It would be embarrassing for you to have to crawl out from under the bed, with Faraday, after the storm was over. I saved you that humiliation."

"How would you know I wasn't helping Faraday divert the path of the storm from right over this very shack and thereby saving our lives?"

"From under the bed?"

"No, no. Out from *underfoot*! If you had to be stepping over me, you just might have broken my concentration, and the storm might very well have blown the shack clear to the Gulf. We're just lucky it was a small storm, and Faraday could handle it all by himself."

The laughter bubbled in her, and she could no longer control it. They laughed, their eyes brimmed with it, as they looked at each other in appreciation. Faraday watched them, then he went over, shoved the screen door open with his nose, and went out to sit on the porch and watch it rain.

Peggy hurried to tidy up after they had finished eating, but Joe looked out the window and said, "It's raining. Why don't we take a nap now and maybe it'll quit raining and we can walk later?'' He shoved his hands into his jean pockets and turned toward her with a bland look on his face. ''If we walk now you'll get your clothes wet.''

Her face fell and she looked woefully out the window before she lifted her chin in determination and said, ''You nap, I'm going now.''

He didn't dare let her go out alone; she might keep walking. ''Well, let me go through the things in the truck again. There ought to be at least one poncho out there.''

There were four. How had he managed to overlook them in the first hunt? He hadn't wanted her to go out walking. The ponchos were all tidily folded into little bags. One was red, and he gave that one to her. Did he think she would take the sandy-green one and vanish? She smiled.

As they started out he warned, ''Watch where you walk.''

She didn't walk, she danced. She was exuberant! She talked and laughed and exclaimed. They went down to the river to inspect it, and she noted that it had risen and was very swift with the rain's overflow. To go west, following the electrical line, she would have to cross the river. How? She pondered that.

He cut a branch the size of his little finger and pencil length; then, with a small stone, he smashed the end against another stone, and it became a rude toothbrush. Not bad. She worked it awkwardly over her fuzzy teeth and ran her tongue around and was delighted.

She looked up and down the riverbed and asked brightly, ''Which are the best fishing holes?'' She felt smug for finding such a clever way to coax him into showing her along the river so she could look for a crossing. Was there a place to ford it, or to jump over it?

There was one possible spot to jump across, but the river tunneled between rocks and it was so swift below that it scared her. Then she saw the bridge. It was homemade of peeled cedar and rope. She affected only casual interest, and that was in the construction. ''How clever,'' she said. ''I wonder who figured this out?''

"I did." As usual he was looking around, keeping everything under his close observation: the weather, the area...her. "The cedar dries as hard as rock. Very durable."

"Are you a carpenter?" What did he do that he could so casually take time off in order to do this frivolous chore for Henry?

"Ummm." He just made the acknowledging sound so she'd know he'd heard her.

"For this place and those materials, it's really very attractive." She wondered if he'd led her there deliberately to show it off to her?

"It serves its purpose."

"And strong." She studied it. "Are you between jobs because you finished one and are going on to another?"

"In a way."

"Joe the jabberer."

He smiled and tucked a strand of her hair back under the hood of her poncho.

"It's marvelous to be out." She smiled back up at him. "Thank you for the moccasins."

"Is being out worth another kiss?" His smile widened, and there was that chipped tooth.

"Perhaps...a small one." She moved to him and lifted her mouth for an ordinary, greeting-type, friendly kiss. It didn't turn out that way. He took her in his arms, and the kiss seemed to steam all the water from the river, making it drip hotly down on them. Their mouths fused and their tongues touched, and it was as if the ponchos weren't between them at all.

His arms were strong and tight around her, holding her to him, and his breath was even hotter than the steamy rain. When he lifted his mouth, they gazed at each other in a bemused trance. Their faces were serious, their pupils enormous, their lips parted in wonder.

It was she who stepped back, she who reluctantly forced her eyes from his, and she who stumbled a little as she put her hand to her head to try to steady herself.

He just stood there, his hand on her arm, holding her steady. He was intent on her, and she was a little flustered. She swallowed and glanced at him, but she tried to avoid his eyes or she would be like a bird trapped by a snake. Not that he was a snake, but she couldn't look away from him—or get away. It scared her.

"We'd better go along," she said.

"Honey..."

"Have you made any other bridges?" She chattered to put the strange moment away from her. "What's down this way? How can you tell if there's quicksand? Does Henry own all this land? What does he do with it? Does he run cattle? Surely not sheep...?"

"A few."

"Sheep? Shame on him. Good God, there's a snake!" It was bleached out and dead.

"It's dead."

"There really *are* snakes." She shivered. "What kind is it?"

"Water moccasin. They're one of the baddies. You avoid them." He pointed over to one side, under a dead bush. "There's a King Coral."

She jumped and clutched at Joe. "Where?"

"See? Just there." It was like a string of jewels, it was so beautifully marked. It was small, and curling its body in agitation. "It was probably flooded out of its home." And he repeated, "Pay attention where you put your feet."

She hadn't even seen the coral snake. She wasn't quite so flippant after that. But they did walk a long way. They finally left the river to go cross-country, and she had no idea where they were. "How can you tell where you're going? There's no sun for direction, and everything looks alike."

"Off to your left, over yonder, is the bluff...."

"Where?"

He drew her closer to him and pointed. "See along my arm?"

"Clear over there?" She frowned. "It doesn't look any different from everything else without the river to measure things against."

"Naturally the river is lower than the surrounding land, so you can't see it from here. It's very easy to get lost. There aren't any houses or roads or road signs."

"You don't get lost."

"Knowing the landmarks is like knowing the streets in a town. After a while you learn them, but even then, you have to pay attention. Anybody can get lost." He did seem to drill that in. "And you have to watch where you walk."

"If you're always watching where you're stepping, you can't look around."

"It's like driving a car: you look ahead, to the sides, and in back of you in the rearview mirror all the time."

"You look beyond, and you turn to look back."

"As I said, this is an isolated place. It pays to be alert."

"You mean...it's dangerous?"

"Probably not."

"*Probably* not?"

"More than likely there's no danger."

"You're a great comfort."

He grinned.

There probably wasn't any danger at all, other than losing her way in a snake-infested land. He was trying to frighten her so she wouldn't try to get away.

She considered him. Really, he was very nice to her. This whole episode could have been ghastly with another man. A lecherous one. Joe was sweet. A gentleman. He had made her the shoes. And he was a tease. He probably thought she expected him to make love to her. With Joe it would never be ravishment. He was too tender. He could make love to any woman he wanted, and she would like it. With Joe, even a professional virgin would probably like it the first time. Joe was special.

"Let's go back to the shack and take a nap." He licked his lower lip, trying to be casual.

He might not ravish her, but he would certainly take advantage of any weakening in her defenses. How wicked of him. Like when she was asleep and he had made love to her. Why hadn't she stopped him sooner? Well, she had been curious to see just how far he would go. And she had found out.

"What's over there?" She ignored his invitation to go back. She knew he really wanted her to climb into a cozy bed with him on a cool, rainy afternoon.

"More of Texas."

"And down that way?"

"Eventually you'd come to Mexico." He tilted his head and the water ran off his Stetson. "Let's go back to the shack."

She was tired. She asked, "How far is it?"

"Just about a mile. We've come in a wide bend, so we've walked farther than that."

"Oh." She hadn't realized they had come so far. She looked around. She didn't want to say okay, because that would sound as if she wanted to...well, as if she were *willing*, so she said, "I suppose we could head in that direction."

They walked in silence. She wasn't skipping and dancing along now. She was watching the ground for snakes. And she was tired. The sandy ground absorbed the rain, then hardened, so it became easier to walk.

"If you see shallow places where the water is standing, go around them. Or soft places. Quicksand is mostly water."

"Have you seen any?"

"A likely place—back a short way."

"Why didn't you tell me?"

"You weren't going to walk into it." He took her arm and moved her a step sideways and something skittered in the wet grass. She said, "Eeeee! What was that?"

"Pack rat."

She turned pale and her head jerked around as her eyes darted.

"It isn't going to hurt you. It's trying to save its treasures from the water."

"A *rat*!"

"Not a slinky, narrow-eyed, city rat. A nice, clean, busy, country rat."

She put a hand to her head.

"See? You're excitable. Now you can understand why I didn't show you the quicksand. You tend to be a bit skittish." He smiled as if he were pleased.

He probably figured he had cured her of any attempts to run away. She realized it wouldn't be easy, and she hoped it wouldn't be necessary. Henry might well have finally shown up.

But only Joe's pickup was there by the shack. "Wouldn't he have waited?" she asked in a discouraged voice.

"He did. He's just inside."

She grinned excitedly and received a quizzical look in return. She exclaimed, "Henry's here!"

"No, no. No, no, no. I thought you meant Faraday." He took her poncho off over her head and hung it on a peg on the porch.

She wilted, dragged into the shack and exclaimed stridently, "Get that dog off the bed!"

"I don't think exercise agrees with you."

"He probably has fleas!"

"Faraday? A.K.C. registered stud? Have you ever seen him scratch?"

"He'd be too lazy to scratch."

Joe lifted Faraday's sagging body off the bed and crooned soothingly to him as he carried him out to the truck, put him inside, and left the door open. Peggy snatched the quilt off the bed and took it outside to shake it angrily. She put it back on the bed and put her soaked moccasins on a heavy towel to dry; then she pulled the bedding into place and made it up, jerking and punching it into place.

Joe came back to the shack, hung his poncho on another peg, opened the door, and tossed his hat inside, then followed it himself. She lifted her chin and said tartly, "Very funny."

"What you need," Joe declared solemnly, "is a lime Popsicle."

Sure. An aphrodisiac. Then, with the dog out of the way so he couldn't watch in critical expertise, Joe would lure her into that squeaky old bed and make it sing. And her too. Why did men always think the way to sweeten a woman's temper was to make love to her? She wondered if it was one of those home remedies that worked.

Thoughtfully she ate the lime Popsicle and waited for the surge of desire to quicken her tired body. Joe was digging around in the cupboards and triumphantly came up with a deck of cards. Cards?

They played gin rummy right through the rest of the day and into the evening. When they had to eat, they ate to one side and continued the bloodthirsty game. They realized their hunger only because Faraday climbed down out of the truck and came to the screen—refreshed from his afternoon nap—and demanded food. That triggered their own hunger.

When they could no longer see the cards and had to quit, they sat and talked about likes, dislikes, opinions, and humor. And Joe remarked thoughtfully in evaluation, "You've got the killer instinct when it comes to card-playing. My God, what a competitive player! There's something terrifying to an innocent country boy like me when a woman slaps down the cards and leans forward like that and smiles that way and says, '*Hah!*' when she wins, with not even a false attempt at good sportswomanship. Scares me to death! I begin to wonder if I'm safe out here all alone with you!"

In the last of the day's faint light she swaggered around the limited space and hooked her thumbs in her belt loops. "I can control my baser instincts. You have nothing to fear from me. You're completely safe."

"If I remember my history rightly, that's what Hitler said to Czechoslovakia. And what Attila the Hun said to—"

"I shall not attack." She lifted an arm to point at the ceiling.

"Something like that, but look what happened!"

She held up a peaceful palm. "I mean that you're perfectly safe."

"Well, damn!" He stood up and towered over her slight figure. "You mean if I crawl into bed I can just go to sleep? I don't have to sit up and cringe in terror at a fate worse than death?"

She put her hand up on his shoulder in a comforting gesture and reassured him. "You may rest in peace."

"Rest in *peace*? You're going to murder me?"

"No. *Sleep!*"

"How about arm-wrestling me for my virtue? Two falls out of three?" He slid his fingers into his back pockets and tilted back on his boot heels, watching her with an almost-hidden, smug expression.

"Just go to bed." She took down "her" shirt, put it around her shoulders, turned her back to him, and began undressing under its covering screen in the first full darkness of the rainy August night. Would he make love to her that night?

He left the shack. She got into bed, clear over against the wall, with her back to the door, and pretended to be sound asleep as she waited for him to come back. Her eyes were open, her pupils enormous as she tried to see in the dark. She could hear the rain still dripping onto the metal roof, and she could hear the leaves of the big oak as they moved in the wind, and the air smelled fresh and clean. The quilt was lovely and snuggly in the coolness of the night, and her body tingled expectantly.

He was gone a long time, and when he returned, he spoke quietly to Faraday on the porch before he opened the door noiselessly; then there was the electrifying rustle of his clothes. She was breathing with probably one-fifth of her lung capacity.

He stood by the bed for a minute before he very quietly lifted the quilt and eased down. He thought she was asleep. She had fooled him. He must be a little stupid if he thought a woman could get to sleep under such circumstances.

She lay there perfectly still, rigid, breathing more quickly, but still using only twenty percent of her potential. Her eyes darted and she clenched her teeth from nerves. How could he possibly be right there *in bed with her* and go to sleep?

He said, "I'd sure like to make love to you, but then I'd have to lie here, kept awake by you crying and whimpering."

"Be...because it would hurt?" she ventured.

"No, no, no, no. Because you'd want more. That's the way it is with virgins. They find out how much fun it is, and how good it feels, and they get greedy. You'd spend the rest of the night pestering me to do it again and again, and I'd never get any sleep." He yawned.

Then he went on, "You've spent the day running me out and around the whole, entire countryside to get me tired, and danged if you haven't. I'm still a growing boy, and I need my sleep, so the smartest thing for me to do is to keep my hands...my...oh, honey, just go to sleep."

"Joe..."

"Do you know, when you say 'Joe' it sets your mouth just exactly right to be kissed?" His voice was husky and a little thready. "But if I turn over and kiss you, all is lost. I would make love to you, and then I'd have to spend the rest of the night fighting you off.

"Men never have a chance. Women are just built so interesting, and they're so soft and pretty and sweet. It's a wonder the whole world isn't knee-deep in crawling babies...."

"It is."

"Well, it isn't *men*'s fault. It's women! They're just so magical. You put your hand on my arm and you paralyze me. Now I know what made the petrified forest. Some woman put her hand on that wood and look what happened! Honey, have a little mercy on me and just go to sleep."

Although she was quiet, she didn't go to sleep for a long, long time. She lay there thinking that he did not want to make love with her. He could have, but he hadn't. He was tactful and kind, so he gave all those excuses. But he probably didn't really want to. He was trapped with her out there in the middle of nowhere, and he was male and she was female, so he might be tempted, but he didn't actually want to. She could make him. And he would. But after it was over, he would regret it.

That thought finally sobered her enough to cool her: he would regret it. She accepted that forlornly, and she wondered what was the matter with her that she couldn't find a man like Joe to love her. She would be an old maid, just like before, and devote herself to other people's babies.

Peggy did sleep, and she dreamed of Joe standing in the middle of the painted desert, petrified, while she stormed around, raging, trying to find the woman who had put her hand on him and ruined him for all womankind.

"Hey!" Joe's frozen figure moved, *and he shattered*! Her frantic fingers tried to reassemble him. "Honey?" His voice must have been released from the fragments, because it coiled deliciously in her ear. "Joe!" she sobbed in regret. And in her ear, the disembodied voice of Joe said, "It's okay, honey." Okay? How could he say so? She wept with despair. "Oh, Joe..."

"Honey, you're just having a nightmare. You're okay."

Her eyes opened into darkness! She touched his blur of an assembled face. His ghost? Then she realized that she had been dreaming.

"Oh, *Joe*!" She flung her arms around him as he kissed her mouth—which had been set exactly right by saying his name.

The dream had sent her into emotional turmoil before her lips ever touched his, so the kiss was a mind-bending, toe-curling meshing of need without any hesitant preliminaries. Her muscles and sinews gave up, making her motions floppy. Her lungs labored as her mouth fed on his. Her hands pushed at him—but independently her backbone arched her against him!

Bodily confusion reigned. That was probably because her mind wasn't functioning. She was operating on emotional need and physical desire, and she wasn't used to allowing herself to behave that way. She had rejected them for so long that she wasn't programmed to cope with their actual occurrence. It was all new, so there were no reference points, and she blundered along, allowing chaos to rule. Poor Joe.

She couldn't get close enough to him. Her kisses were frantic, hungry, deep, unstinting. She wiggled closer, moving against him erotically, her shirt undone—and he cooperated.

His big hands slid where they wanted, where he wanted, where she ached for them. His arms crushed her to him, and she moaned and gasped and carried on, outrageously wanton.

Her bold fingers went their errant way, her palms sliding over his sweat-filmed back, up his head and into his thick hair. Then they went down to his chest and farther, and though she blushed, her fingers went their way.

Joe gasped and groaned and jerked and writhed under her freely roaming, adventuring fingers. He sucked air through his teeth and his lungs whooshed it out. And the tangle of their encounter was giving the bed springs a joyous ride.

The jolt that stopped her was his hard palm pressing against her hot core. It stopped her cold. No other man's hand had ever been there, and it shocked her. She stiffened, she froze, and her mind seized control again.

After a minute Joe's husky voice asked, "Cooler heads prevail?" But he moved that palm in a hard caress before he slowly made it withdraw, but then he slid it around to her back and pulled her tightly to him as he groaned, his arms as hard as steel and his muscles like iron. She might well have turned him to stone!

"Oh, Joe..." She was appalled, and so embarrassed.

"Shhhh," he soothed her, trying to control his breathing and his trembling body.

"I'm sorry."

"It's okay." He had to swallow.

"I had a dream..."

"It must have been a dandy." Humor laced through his roughened voice.

"I dreamed you were petrified."

"That's not far wrong."

"And you shattered!"

"I just might."

"And I was trying to put you back together."

He laughed.

She was so emotionally disorganized and unsatisfied that she cried, and he had to comfort her for a while. Then, as her crying eased, he loosened his hold on her and said regretfully, "I have to go outside."

"Oh. Sure. Go ahead. I'm all right now. I'm so sorry, Joe. I don't know what happened."

"I'm going to live. But just barely."

Barely? "No," she advised earnestly. "You'd better wear clothes. I don't think I'm too reliable."

He tousled her sweat-dampened hair and kissed her forehead. "Joe. We could—"

"Better not." He moved to leave the bed.

She put a hand on his shoulder. "There's a name for men like you who tease and then won't."

"Careful." He leaned to kiss her mouth.

She was silent. He hesitated; then he took a bracing breath, left the bed and went out the door and into the rain.

When Peggy woke up it was barely light. She listened and heard only the sound of paper faintly rustling. She slitted her eyes and saw Joe, dressed, leaning over the table, writing something. Then he looked over at her in the dim morning light, came to the side of the bed, and very, very gently touched his palm to the side of her head. He straightened, walked quietly out of the shack, over to the truck, and drove away! He was leaving her there!

She flipped back the quilt, scrambled out of the bed, and snatched up the paper to squint in the dim light to read. "By the time you read this, I'll be back."

Well, he *was* coming back. He had probably gone to see why Henry hadn't come and released him from woman-sitting her. He was tired of this foolishness. Propinquity was getting to him. She was beginning to look good to him, and he knew he had to get away. How depressing.

She had finally found a man she would be willing to try making love with, and he wasn't really interested. He sure had pretended well. She had always heard that men could be easily triggered. The surprise was how interested *she* was. Could it be propinquity for her, too? Just the isolation, the Eden-like situation? If she saw Joe under normal circumstances, would he be as attractive? As sexual?

She dressed pensively, and then she looked for her moccasins. She looked everywhere. They weren't there. Where could they be? She stood up and impatiently put her hands on her hips and looked around the shack. They weren't anywhere around. He had taken them! He had gone off and taken her moccasins with him! He *expected* her to try to get away!

Of all the things to do. He didn't trust her one bit! He had left her there and taken the moccasins with him so she couldn't get away! Her temper flared, and she paced the room and slammed things around as she fixed herself something to eat. And she fumed as she chewed. It had quit raining. Sometime during the night the rain had stopped. She could escape. She would show him.

She put on her suit, fixed a sandwich to take along in case it took her until noon to find a house along the electrical line, and she put it and a jar of water in her shoulder bag. Then she slid her feet into the discarded sleeves from her suit jacket, tore more material from the de-hemmed sheet and wrapped the sleeves firmly in place. She stood up, and they seemed to be just fine. She walked back and forth, and decided they really weren't bad.

She slathered herself with sunscreen, tied the bandanna around her head, and made up the bed. She looked around. Then, very firmly, she closed the door and stalked off toward the bridge, to cross the river and follow the homemade electric line to freedom.

Faraday rolled an eye up at her as she went past, and she said brusquely, "Goodbye, Faraday," as she strode off toward the river.

Faraday wuffed, but she didn't look back. As she neared the river she heard him bark. And when she went out of sight, he howled. He was probably afraid of being alone.

She crossed the river, then had to find her way up the bluff. That took a while. From the top she looked around, but she saw no sign of the shack. Then she had to relocate the electrical wire which was her guide to civilization.

She found it and set out on her westward trek. The area she crossed had been sheep-grazed. There were mesquite trees, as in most of southeastern Texas, and the kind of cactus that looked like plates stacked on top of each other to make an interesting pile of spiny barriers.

She had to stop and resecure her "shoes" several times, but it was still better than going barefooted. She slowed her pace at sunrise. Faintly, far away, she could still hear Faraday.

There were no houses. Nothing to indicate that the world was overpopulated. Perhaps the rooster she had heard really had been a wild Texas bush rooster. She had only heard it that one morning. It might have been eaten by the pond alligators...or a puma. She looked around. It was calm, and there was no sign of anything like civilization. It was completely deserted. Wild. What impulsive foolishness had caused her to leave the shack?

The sun grew hot. She found some shade just off her trail, sat down to rest and allowed herself a sip or five of water. Maybe she should have brought two jars of water. She could no longer hear Faraday.

She got up and trudged on as the sun inched higher...or the horizon dipped lower. Joe was an interesting man. Had he returned to the shack? What would he think when he found she was gone? Would he say, "Good riddance"? What if he followed her? Why should he?

It was possible that he would be very, very angry. He had been assigned to cope with her, and she had gotten away. It would irritate him. He might very well follow. She looked back over her shoulder and hurried her steps a little, glancing back often.

Every so often she would stop and look back along her trail, and then she would have to remember to turn and go on. She was getting tired. It must be noon. She squinted at the sun which she was sure would be overhead—but it was still only about two hours up from the horizon.

Her watch said it was nine, but she wasn't sure she had wound it. It might have stopped. She wound it then, but there was no way to know if it had stopped for several hours and was starting from the completely wrong spot.

There was a way to tell time by putting a stick in the ground and seeing where its shadow fell, but she wasn't sure just how that worked. She was hungry. How far had she come? Where was Joe? She would probably die out there, and the sun would turn her into leather, if the buzzards left anything. Buzzards? She looked up. They weren't circling yet.

She sat down in some lacy shade provided by a mesquite and allowed herself another sip of water. It had been brilliant of her to remember to bring water. She hadn't realized another house would be so far away. What if it was another weekend shack and no one was there? What day was today? She had been with Joe...was it three days? Four. That would make this...only Tuesday? What had she done to so recklessly take off in a snit because she'd lost her temper? What was she doing out there?

She heard it: barking! *It was a dog pack*! The dogs had caught her scent and were on her trail! She panicked, got up, and looked for a tree she could climb. The dog pack was after her! She would be surrounded, and they would lunge in and hamstring her, and she would fall, and they would be on her, tearing her throat—and eating her. What had she done?

Her breath rasped in her throat. She looked back along her trail and couldn't see them yet. She ran and fell, and by a miracle her jar of water wasn't broken.

She scrambled up and deliberately calmed herself. She searched her surroundings for a fortress...and saw the cactus. It was the dinnerplate variety, and it had grown very high, and the depth of the copse was impressive. It was impenetrable. She closed her mind to what creatures might be harbored inside it, lurking there, and she edged her way in very, very carefully. The spines were sharp and could fester, and she could die there of gangrene.

She waited. That took a great deal of courage, because dogs terrified her on city streets when they were attached to a human by a strong leash. To wait to face a pack of wild dogs was the epitome of bravery in her mind. It surpassed anything she had ever forced herself to do. But she shivered as she sound came closer.

Faraday came into sight. He had joined the pack! How like a dog! He lumbered forward howling, leading them to her!

No other dog showed up. She waited and watched, but it was just Faraday. He eventually got to the cactus, stopped, and looked at her. She returned the look.

He had gone back to the wild. Like the rooster. In animals, the veneer of civilization was very thin. They reverted easily. Faraday was the beginning of a wild dog pack!

How could she possibly be afraid of him? How could she be afraid of a dog that whined for more syrup on his pancakes? He sat down, panting, then flopped over as if he'd had a heart attack.

Eight

Peggy eased forward out of the cactus and leaned over the dog. He whimpered pitifully, his tongue lolling out. He was dying of thirst.

He couldn't drink from the jar and, even if he could, she did not want to have to drink after him. She went through her purse and found a handkerchief with tatted lace edges. She was very reluctant to use *that* handkerchief to moisten the dog's mouth, but she did it.

She straightened and, as if he could understand, she said to the dog, "Get up. I will not carry you around. I'm not Joe. I'm leaving. If you want to come along, you'll have to get up and walk." And she started off.

She trudged out of sight, and the dog wailed. She shouted back, "Come on or be quiet." Dumb, cowardly dog. And he was a stud! How appalling to perpetrate such genes.

She heard a horrible sound and whipped around to face a hound of hell, but it was only Faraday huffing along after her. When she stopped, he stopped and flopped over again. "If you exercised a little now and then, a stroll in the countryside wouldn't be so horrendous. Get up!''

She started off again, he followed, and they went grimly on. The wire continued relentlessly west. What had she done? What was she doing out there all alone? Finally she admitted she was grateful for the dog's company. She allowed her steps to slow a little to accommodate him, but he only slowed his and tended to sit down, and then he had to catch up.

They had to keep moving. If they stopped no one would ever find them. They had to go on until they found someone to help them out of this god-awful situation. She could go back to the shack. She considered that as she plodded on.

The snort was so ominous that it stopped her in her tracks. Faraday became alert and tense. All that flab could be tense? That was rather amazing. She watched the rigid dog and listened, but she heard nothing more. However Faraday was still very, very alert, and his tension spooked Peggy.

The second snort was followed by a chuffing sound. One chuff like a steam train. And then she saw the bull. It was dun-colored, with very large horns. It was intimidatingly big, and there was no fence between her and it.

Her heart squeezed up into her windpipe and stayed there, a dead lump. She opened her mouth and screamed. But the sound of her scream was pitifully thin in that vast nothingness.

The bull was a solid, enormous, *dangerous* reality, and she was puny in contrast. What in God's name was she doing out there?

If anything happened to her, Francine would never forgive herself and would spend the rest of her days in grieving regret. For Francine's sake Peggy knew she had to survive. She straightened up, facing the bull in her bright, blindingly purple suit, and she considered what she could do. She was so afraid that her ears hummed like a motorboat.

Faraday set up one hell of a roaring and he *advanced*, bristling, to stand between her and the bull! Faraday? She was distracted by that. The humming got louder in her head, and she figured that the magnitude of her situation was more than she could take, and that her skull was probably going to explode.

The bull chuffed and lowered its head, scraping one forefoot back. Faraday snarled and danced from side to side in challenge. Faraday? Peggy backed up cautiously, then panicked and ran, screaming in terror.

The bull roared, the dog barked savagely low and dreadfully serious, and Peggy fled pell-mell, shrieking. Then she stopped as the dog gave a sharp whimper! She turned back abruptly. The bull had flung Faraday aside and was standing still, watching the dog scramble to its feet. Once again Faraday growled furiously and danced to attract the bull.

Faraday would be killed! She took off her shirt and waved it at the bull, and he turned his huge, dangerous head her way! Her conduct was so unutterably mad that the roaring filled her brain, and she could no longer hear perfectly. Despite the roar, she *could* hear the dog growling and see him dancing, and she could hear the bull bellowing as it put back its humungous head and challenged the entire world—but especially that lump of a dog and that stick of a woman.

She ran, the bull charged her, and Faraday nipped the bull's back leg and distracted it—and suddenly the roar in her ears became a blue pickup all tangled up in the whole mess, and she saw Joe's face absolutely *livid* with fury!

He slid the pickup to a stop between her and the bull, and the bull hesitated a bit, then came on and smashed into the off-side of the truck in a blind temper. The dog snarled and Joe yelled to Peggy, "*Get in!*" as he slung himself out of the cab and over onto the bed of the truck. He swept up a rope and sent it hissing just *that fast,* hooked it around the bull's head...and then Joe fastened his end of the rope to a part of the tripod on the truck bed.

On wet-noodle legs, and with every muscle jerking and every nerve hysterical, Peggy climbed into the cab and burst into tears. Faraday got in beside her, panting, pretty full of himself, and she wrapped her arms around him and wept into his doggy-smelling coat.

Joe got back into the truck and didn't even speak to her. His color was high, his movements were harsh, and he shot the gears into place roughly, but then he eased the truck along, towing the bull, who was not willing.

"Joe—"

"Don't you say one word to me! I'm only just barely controlling a very violent urge to throttle you! How could you do such a thing? Don't answer me. I don't want to hear you honey your way out of this! Do you realize what all could have happened to you? I've never seen such a mule-headed, unmanageable woman in my entire life!

"Going off that way and leaving me to go crazy thinking about the things that could have happened to you. How dare you? Be quiet! There's nothing that you can say that will get you out of this in one piece!" His eyes flashed briefly to her, shooting sparks, he was so angry.

Her gratitude began to seep out of her to be easily replaced by temper. Here she had just endured this horrendous episode and *he* was mad at *her*! She gave him an indignant stare then said, "Now just a—"

"I said for you to hush! Don't you say a word! It's only my completely rigid self-discipline that's keeping me from turning you over my knee and tanning your bottom until you wouldn't be able to sit down for a week! Of all the moronic—"

She snapped, "I beg your pardon—"

"You'd do well to do just that, but I prefer that you just sit there with your mouth shut while you think for a change. Do you have any idea what you've..."

He went on and on, and in the meantime Faraday had wiggled around between them and was sitting on the seat backward, with his front paws on the top of the seat back. He was laughing out the rear cab window at the antics of the reluctant bull being coerced into following the truck. Faraday couldn't leave well enough alone, and he gave a snide bark or two. The bull didn't like that, and he bellowed, shook his head, and plowed into the back end of the truck.

Joe bellowed too. "Hush!" he yelled in an unfriendly way to Faraday and commanded him, "Get down!" Faraday was offended.

Joe continued his tirade at Peggy, but Faraday didn't get down on the cab floor as directed. He turned around, pulled in his tongue, gave Joe an aloof look and crowded away from Joe and closer to Peggy. Joe was unkind enough not to notice that.

It was only a couple of hundred feet from where she had encountered the bull that the electric wire split. One strand went on west but the other turned south, and Joe took the south turn. There—in sight—was a rustic house in a lovely pool of shade under some pecan trees. Beyond it a windmill was desultorily turning, and below was the farm pond. In another few minutes she would have made good her escape. She had been that close to freedom.

However, it appeared that Joe was taking her to that house, so she would be able to ask for sanctuary anyway. Anyone would give her protection once she explained her position. She sat straighter, and then she remembered that her poisonously purple skirt was back there somewhere, on the ground and abandoned.

"I don't have my skirt."

Joe gave her a snarling look.

"When the bull charged, I threw it at him."

Joe flinched, and he said through his teeth, "Why in God's name did you wave it at the bull?" He spaced the words, as if she might have trouble figuring them out.

"He'd already flipped Faraday once and was waiting to try again."

"My God..." But he didn't finish what God was supposed to hear.

As they drew up to the rustic house—which was whole leaps up the housing scale from the shack—a man of Hispanic lineage came out of another truck and yelled, "Joe!"

But Joe interrupted with a string of unintelligible Spanish words, and whatever he said, it caused the man's face to sober and look puzzled as he sought to see who else was in Joe's truck. Since Peggy didn't speak Spanish, and the words Joe used were not from her limited range of tortilla, enchilada, and tostada, she had no idea what he had said.

Joe eased his truck to a full stop, and the man walked over to Joe's side of the cab as he grinned back toward the bull, which was shaking its head trying to get rid of Joe's rope. The man asked a question, and Joe replied at some length. The man slapped a friendly hand on Joe's arm, said something else and went away.

"What's—" Peggy began.

"I told you to be quiet." Joe wasn't kidding at all.

With his attitude, she doubted he was in any mood to reply to any of her questions, so she decided it would be a waste of time to try to ask them. She struggled to get Faraday to move over and give her more room, but he too was mad at Joe for speaking so impolitely to him and continued to crowd her.

At that moment the screen door of the house burst open and the yard was soon filled with four or five little black-eyed kids, who laughed and pointed and exclaimed. The man cautioned them to stay back. His gestures were eloquent, so Peggy didn't have to understand his words.

He had come back carrying a long pole. Now he approached the bull, and the bull backed up, but the man was quick and clamped a ring onto the bull's nose, removed the rope from his neck and, talking as soothingly as Joe used to talk to Faraday, he led the bull away.

A young, pregnant woman came out of the house and waved. Joe immediately called out to her in Spanish. She said something back, cautioned the kids, and went back inside.

Joe shifted the truck into reverse and swung around, heading back the way they had come.

"Where...?"

He silenced her with one look.

They drove back to the encounter area, and Joe sighted and retrieved the vile purple skirt. He held it up, glared in his inspection of the trampled cloth, snapped it several times to get rid of the dust, and got back into the truck to thrust it at her.

Since she was sitting there in blue-and-green panties and the jacket whose sleeves were tied untidily to her feet, she supposed she should be grateful for the return of the skirt, but it went hard for her to scrape up more than an icy, "Thank you." She shoved at Faraday to get some room, but he simply leaned on her as she wriggled into the skirt.

Perhaps it was the expending of temper in snapping the cloth so vigorously, or maybe it was seeing the torn place in the skirt that had been cut by the sharp hoof of the bull, but Joe's reply was almost civil. "Anytime."

Silent, they returned to the rustic house, got out, and were surrounded by darling children, all of whom spoke in a shrieking jumble of lovely Spanish sounds with a good deal of pointing in all directions and lots of giggling and dancing-eyed glances at Peggy.

Joe touched the children's heads in obvious fondness and gestured as he explained. *Toro* was one word he used, and that meant bull. So the children were talking about the bull.

The man returned, grinning widely, glancing at Peggy and talking to Joe in a questioning tone. Joe replied. Then Joe said shortly to Peggy, "The kids have been held inside the house while the bull was loose, and Ramon is glad you found him. He's a gentle bull—practically a family pet."

Peggy gave him a disbelieving glance.

Joe added, "This is Ramon Gonzales, a friend of Henry's and mine." Then he turned to Ramon and said quite a lot, too much to be simply giving her name in turn, and Peggy heard "Margarita." He hadn't introduced her as Francine!

Ramon took off his hat and bowed slightly, with a big grin, then launched into a long speech that rolled pleasingly from his tongue.

Joe explained. "Ramon thanks you for finding his bull." Ramon laughed, so Joe said something else to Ramon, who rubbed his hand over his mouth, turned, and called toward the house.

The woman reappeared, and Joe aimed a long string of lovely sounds at her. She frowned as she came over to them and questioned the men as she studied Peggy.

Joe gestured and insisted on something. She shook her head and gave Joe a doubting look. But Joe turned to Peggy and said, "This is Ramon's wife, Teresa." Then he said "Margarita" again in the midst of an undecipherable bunch of sentences.

The woman smiled at Peggy and nodded once to acknowledge the introduction and Peggy's carefully enunciated "How do you do?" Then Teresa continued to question and argue with Joe.

Finally Joe said something that caused Teresa to tilt back her head and say "Ahhhh," while Ramon laughed.

"What did you say?" Peggy asked in a starchy way.

"I said we've had a lovers' quarrel and you ran away from me."

Peggy blew up. She snapped at Joe and explained carefully to the Gonzaleses, with accompanying sweeping gestures, "I've been held prisoner by this man! Just look at me! Look at this suit! Would any free woman willingly wear it?" She paused for dramatic effect.

Joe translated their replies. "Teresa says the color is delightful and she envies you the suit, but why did you put the sleeves on your feet?"

"He stole my shoes!" She flung out her arms.

Joe translated that in some complicated way, but it took a long time, and Peggy watched avidly as they all exchanged a torrent of words. Then Joe turned back and told Peggy, "She said 'oh.'" And the Gonzaleses laughed.

She should have taken Spanish. She told Joe, in an accusing tone, "You have no shame."

He smiled. She realized that he had become more cheerful as the conversation with the Gonzaleses had progressed. He held one or another of the children and hugged each one in turn. From the looks of it, Teresa had had a child a year for five years, and this would be the sixth. That was entirely too many children in too short a period of time.

"Tell her about birth control," Peggy advised Joe. "Be as tactful as you can." The last was said during a burst of chatter between the couple, followed by their laughter.

"Don't you think that would be intruding on someone else's life?" Joe inquired politely.

"That hasn't slowed you down from intruding on *my* life! Have you considered that? Tell her she's probably extremely deficient in calcium, and if she continues having all these babies, she'll probably lose her teeth."

Joe spoke to Teresa, who smiled broadly and exhibited her good, sound teeth. Joe explained to Peggy, "I said you thought she had pretty teeth." Somehow that caused more smiles and chuckles.

"She won't have *any* if she keeps on having kids every year." Then Peggy pointed as she counted slowly and distinctly, "One, two, three, four, five and," pointing to Teresa's protruding stomach, "six?"

Teresa nodded and laughed. *"Seis."*

"This one will be named Seis?" Peggy asked Joe.

"Seis is six."

Peggy pinned Teresa with a stern look and counted the kids again, then shook her finger and her head, and said, "No, no, no, no." She did realize, though, that this was a possibly confusing and not very explicit birth-control lecture.

Teresa smiled tolerantly and smoothed her hand proudly over her protruding belly before she gestured that Peggy was to follow her. It was then that Peggy noticed the Gonzales dog acting like a groupie for bull-chasing Faraday, and Faraday was smiling and holding his head up in a boasting way. The stance also kept his ears off the ground.

As Peggy moved to follow Teresa, her right foot stepped on some loose fabric from her left "shoe" and she stumbled. Joe must have been keeping close watch on her, because he moved swiftly to steady her. "Wait a minute," he said, then went back to the blue pickup and returned *with her moccasins!*

In handing her the moccasins he refreshed her memory as to just exactly why she was where she was and why she had gone through such a trying day: he had stolen the moccasins in the first place! She took them from him, her lips thin, and her eyes narrowed and glaring. "How kind of you to return them," she said with sarcastic venom.

Joe smiled as if he would have liked to pat her bottom in a very sassy way. Shocking man. She flicked a glance at Ramon and Teresa and saw that they were smiling at her and Joe with indulgent humor. Peggy was sure then that she should have taken Spanish instead of French. There was more to life than reading menus.

Of course, as they jabbered away in their language, she could offer comments in French, but it wouldn't make any difference. French would be equally incomprehensible to them as her English. People who lived in this country should speak the language, she decided. It would certainly make *her* life a lot easier.

Teresa led Peggy to one of the rockers on the cool porch and brought her a glass of lemonade and a wet towel. It was heaven. She rubbed the towel slowly over her face, then down her neck and along her arms.

The pleasure of the cool wetness was almost hedonistic in that heat and after the encounter with the bull. Faraday's bravery had been a real surprise.

She looked around for the dog and saw that he was generously rewarding the groupie for her admiration...and without a fee. Faraday was having an unusual day. Perhaps he really was reverting to native behavior. Was his attention to the bitch generosity? No, he was simply seeding his own dog pack.

Before today Peggy would never have believed Faraday capable of hunting, much less defending someone. Appearances could be deceiving. And Peggy recalled the savage sound of his snarl as he had challenged the bull. She had been out there alone facing that raw primal violence—and it was all Joe's fault.

As she bent to remove the suit jacket sleeves from her feet, Joe moved over to her. Still talking to Ramon, he sat easily on the edge of the porch and took her foot in his hands.

How dare he? His big, strong, square hands made her foot look small and helpless. Ramon stood relaxed, hands on his hips, while Teresa sat in the other rocker. Peggy tried to pull her foot away from Joe, but he easily countered that. It would be too unladylike to kick him with the other foot, so she held still, grimly enduring his ministrations.

As he talked easily to the Gonzaleses, he began to unwind the mess of fabric she had struggled with all morning. The sleeves were dirty and ragged, and looking at them touched her heart with self-pity.

He bared her poor little foot—the toenails bright with coral polish—and he moved his big rough hands over it with incredible gentleness as he inspected it for cuts and bruises.

He turned and looked up at her from the shadow of his Stetson, and his eyes were so kind and gentle that a tear crept out to tremble on her lower lashes! She had thought that only Francine could do that. Peggy blinked, knowing the tear looked vulnerable, and *she* was invincible, but it clung there. To wipe it off would appear weak, so she ignored it.

Joe licked his upper lip and his hands on her feet were so nice. Erotic. Good heavens! How could she possibly be disturbed by this man's hands on her foot after her morning's ordeal had been caused by him!

And with a yard full of kids right there as a very visual lesson in the residual effects of eroticism? Just look at Teresa! Ramon had Teresa out there all alone, with no neighbors, and more than likely no television, and there was nothing else to do! Six minutes with the man and Teresa got nine months of baby. Peggy hardened her heart.

But then Joe took that cool, wet towel and he massaged her calf and cleaned her foot with a tenderness that faded the nine-month part to an inconsequential blur and brought the six minutes into very sharp focus. Women's minds worked in strange ways.

Peggy forced herself to count the children having a hilarious time in the yard, running and toddling, laughing and squealing, oblivious to Faraday and his companion. Actually it wasn't the children she should be watching, but that groupie. Dumb bitch.

Finally Joe put a moccasin on her cleaned, inspected...cosseted foot. Peggy watched him, and she remembered his cutting Henry's moccasins down to fit her so that she could have a long, lovely, drizzly stroll around the countryside...with him. Men were clever. She mused over the fact that men were inventively tricky specifically to entrap women.

Joe set about giving equal—although separate—time to her other foot. Her first foot didn't get jealous and try to distract him from giving attention to the second one. It rested, relaxed, contented, like a woman in a harem who has already received her share of the sultan's attentions.

Still talking idly to Ramon, Joe thoroughly comforted the second foot and slid the second moccasin in place. Then he came up on the porch, leaned against one of the four-by-fours that supported the porch roof behind Peggy and, as if distracted, slowly removed Peggy's scarf and toyed with her hair.

Still talking with Ramon and Teresa, and occasionally giving Peggy a brief replay of their conversation, he continued to gently untangle her hair. Finally he took his pocket comb and drew it through the silken mass until it lay tamed and gleaming...as contented as her feet.

"You do that very well." She wondered how many women's heads and feet had received his care. The thought made her a bit prickly.

"It's a natural talent," Joe admitted.

"I imagine so." She felt pricklier.

"You ought to see me take the burrs out of a horse's tail."

Peggy had to grin up at Joe.

By then Ramon was sitting on the edge of the porch by his wife, one of his hands absentmindedly caressing Teresa's ankle. It was just a good thing Teresa was already pregnant, Peggy thought.

Lying back in the chair, she began to rock a little, and she found she was smiling at the children's antics, but just beyond them was Faraday, intently concentrating on the willing bitch.

Before she realized what her tongue was doing, she murmured to Joe, "No fee." It appalled her to say it aloud, but she thought he would assume she had meant for his ministering to her.

But he replied softly, "It's his day off."

Her eyes darted to the Gonzaleses, but they hadn't heard. They were exchanging a sly smile, oblivious to everything else.

Joe and Peggy were invited to stay for lunch, and Joe helped Ramon set up a plank table under the pecan trees in the breeze which reached them from the Gulf. Lunch was casual, and the gentle wind was lovely.

They had chili with beans and rice, tortillas dripping with butter, iced tea and lemonade, and an icy watermelon. Peggy helped to feed the smallest ones, and decided it was just as well they were outside. The juicy, sticky watermelon dripped all over everything...the table, the chairs and all the kids. The babies squished the melon between their fat little fingers and giggled as the cool juice ran down their arms and onto their round bellies.

Teresa and Peggy stripped the wiggling, giggling little ones, and Joe and Ramon herded the passel of children over to the windmill, where they dipped buckets of sun-warmed water from the barrel and tipped it over the squealing, naked children.

The two men carried the smallest ones back to the house, with the rest hopping along on the flagstones so their feet wouldn't get sandy again, and the whole bunch were put down for naps.

After that Joe and Peggy said their goodbyes, and Peggy said, "Gracious," badly mispronouncing her thanks. As Joe man-handled a reluctant Faraday into the back of the truck, the Gonzaleses intentionally slurred their own expressions of thanks for the return of the bull, so she wouldn't be embarrassed by the fact of her mistake.

Peggy smiled, still unconvinced that the bull was really gentle and had never hurt anyone. There was that long rip in her skirt from a hoof, and they had kept the kids inside until the bull was again caught.

Joe climbed into the cab with her, and they called a last goodbye. Peggy snapped around, suddenly alert, and demanded, "Did they say '*Mulholland*'?"

"I didn't hear that."

"I thought I heard Ramon say 'Mulholland.'"

"I don't think so."

"Well, I did. And I have no use for anyone by that name."

"Interesting," he said pleasantly, but offered nothing more.

"Why didn't Ramon catch the bull by himself?" She watched their progress along the rough track.

"He'd just realized it had broken through the fence and put the kids in the house when I got there, and then we heard the uproar. He'd just gotten his truck started when we got back."

"What were you doing at their house?"

"I was going to ask them to help find you. You dunderhead. I can't tell you how I felt when I got back to the shack and found you gone! I knew you didn't have your shoes." With his accelerating words she knew his anger was rising again.

He went on. "Just the fact that you had no shoes...! And then all the dangers! When I got back, Faraday was beside himself. My fault entirely. I'd told him to stay. I hadn't told him to guard you, and you'd walked off, and he couldn't do a thing. It never occurred to me you'd do anything so harebrained. Faraday could go straight across the river, but the truck couldn't. I had to follow the road all the way back to the ford."

"I've had as much of you as I intend to take!"

"It wasn't just your actual walking, but what all you'd run into, and when I heard you scream! My God..." Amazingly, he had finally run out of words and took a long pause. "Don't you *ever* do anything like that to me again as long as we live, do you hear me?"

"It would be very simple to solve all your problems." Her voice was quavery. "Let me go."

"No." He was brief about it. Then he smiled as he drove along. "I'm going to take you back to the shack and make love to you for a week. Then we'll have a little food and water and get back to it for another week. After a month or two I'll let you dress occasionally, and after the third kid is born I might let you go back into town now and then." He gave her a hot look, and his grin was wide and white—except for that tiny chip.

A shocking thrill stretched into every cell of her torso and various and sundry appendages. She bit her lower lip and looked out the truck window with fogged eyes, trying to make her lungs perform in a respectable manner.

He stopped the truck and turned off the motor. She studied the expanse of nothing but cactus and mesquite; then she looked at him.

He put one arm along the back of the seat and put his other wrist on the top of the steering wheel as he leaned toward her. His face was serious as he said softly, "I can't wait any longer to kiss you. Come here."

She couldn't move, but he apparently didn't expect her to, for he loomed over her, moving along the seat a little and simply enclosing her. She tried not to respond, a perfect example of an exercise in futility. Her entire system yearned for him. Her lips parted softly, and he kissed her.

She turned immediately to jelly, and he did a magnificent job of keeping her together and reasonably upright by assiduously using his arms, his hands, and his body...and his mouth. It was all extremely lovely and very unfair.

He was so committed to keeping her in the semblance of the female shape that he undid her buttons and worked the basic material. Obviously it *was* work. His breath was labored, and he groaned over the demands on him, but he kept at it with a laudable perseverance.

He worked her so hard that she sighed under his buffeting, her jellied bones constantly threatening to collapse. But he prevailed and won the day...and her.

She was half naked by then. His hat was gone, his shirt somewhere else, and she had her hands on him. He blew out a blast of hot air from laboring lungs and, red-eyed, looked at her. "I don't want our first time to be on the seat of a pickup."

That confused her. What was wrong with that? She tried to understand, gave up, and lifted her mouth to his as her hands tugged him closer.

"Not here," he panted.

"I've decided I'll help."

"I suspected that." His voice trembled, and his words were unsteady. "We'll get married, honey."

"Married? Don't be silly." She nipped along his jaw, slid her arms around his neck and hung from his resisting body as he tried to separate them.

"I've had you out here for almost a week. Your reputation is shot to hell. I'll make the supreme sacrifice and make an honest woman out of you."

"Don't be ridiculous. We'll have some fun, you can teach me how, and leave it at that. Who'd ever know? The Gonzaleses don't speak English. Henry won't tell. He never remembers gossip, so who's to find out?"

Wickedly, Joe smiled. "I'll tell."

And he would! "You wouldn't!"

"You'll be a scarlet woman, and no decent man would have you. I'll do the honorable thing and marry you."

He had lifted himself higher, but she still hung from him, her arms clutched around his shoulders, and in *that* position she said, "I really don't know you very well, and I don't want to get married. This lack of frigidity may be a fluke, like conduct away from home on vacation. I am basically frigid."

"You're a one-man woman, and I'm the man."

"Nonsense."

"You're plainly gorgeous. Your body is—"

"How could anyone possibly be *plainly* gorgeous?"

"It's plain to see you're gorgeous."

"I suppose lying here right before your eyes is pretty plain. Do I shock you?"

"Something sure as hell's going on. You do all sorts of things to me. And I want more." His voice was low and husky.

"Do you really want *me*, Joe? Or do you still think I'm Francine, and this is some kind of revenge against Henry? Are you asking a ransom for me? That is, for Francine? You must realize that Henry knows you don't have Francine, and he may never show up."

"I'll add another room to the house and—"

"House?" she questioned. "How can you call that a house?"

"...And screen the front porch..." He leaned his head down, bracing his body so that only the hair on his chest touched her nipples, and he kissed her again. It was a leisurely, slowly exploring kiss that was mesmerizing. She forgot what they were talking about.

After a time she said, "I don't think there's any real argument against the first time being on the seat of a pickup."

"This is pure unadulterated torment." He gave her another of his alluring kisses. "We'll go back to the shack pretty soon now."

"Now?"

"Shhhhh, you temptress."

"How can you call me a temptress when I was just riding along in this truck, looking out the window, minding my own bus—"

He kissed her again, moving his chest just a little and exciting her with the abrasiveness of his chest hair against her extremely sensitive breasts.

Into his mouth she breathed the words, "You're torturing me."

"Good. You've driven me out of my mind this whole past week."

"Four days."

"An eternity. Don't you feel it? You're the other half of me, and I'm the other half of you. Our minds and bodies are made to fit together like the halves of an orange."

"A lopsided orange. Kiss me."

"Willingly." He groaned the word and complied. "Oh, my love. I must have you. Never tell our kids we initiated our lives together on the front seat of the pickup. Promise." He kissed her more deeply, and she ran her tongue lightly over the chip in his tooth as her hands explored. "I'll have it bronzed," he promised.

A flashing parade of bronzable things flashed through her mind. "What!" she asked in fright.

"The pickup. I'll have it bronzed as a memorial."

"Oh," she agreed with some relief.

After that, thinking vanished and only sensual awareness ruled. Their bodies worshiped each other; their hands and mouths were greedily loving, caressing, fondling.

"Oh, Joe." She said that in quite a lot of remarkable ways—in gasps and moans and sighs. For a frigid woman and a professional virgin, her conduct was really rather astonishing.

His comments were fragmented because he couldn't stop making love to her long enough to cope with a reasonable conversation. He said things like, "I love you...oh, darling...honey, be careful...hold still...ahhhhh...when you were gone I...oh, yes...you like that...my God...easy, easy...don't ever leave me...hear me?"

She just kept saying, "Oh, Joe," which put her mouth exactly right to be kissed.

"You okay...how's that...all right?...oh, honey...oh, my love...you all right?...easy now...honey, wait a little...hold still...don't move...wait...my God!"

The sensations in her body went completely wild. It was so amazing that she could feel such thrills, such skitterings of pleasure, of desire, of longing, of demand. She wanted him so badly that she helped all she could, with her arms holding, her hands smoothing and stroking.

And as her mouth and body and hands drew marvelous responses from him, her body was reacting to his loving of her, as he petted and kneaded and smoothed and kissed her, rubbing against her, sliding along, suckling, licking, and teasing.

She urged her own surrender before he was sure she was ready, but she was writhing with need, and he was convincible. There was her hesitation over whether his assurance that they would fit like the two halves of an orange was really true, but he did fit into her, they joined, and it was magical.

He held her still as long as he could control her, but she moved and squirmed and lifted her hips, and no man could endure such torture for too long before he was tempted to aid in his own undoing.

He made it beautiful for her there on the front seat of the pickup. He used his hands and body to help hers, and he was patient and allowed her mounting excitement full reign until her need went wild—and then he took her to paradise.

Collapsed, they lay panting, murmuring unintelligible sounds, stroking feeble fingers in light caresses, kissing shoulders and throats, sighing, smiling.

"I thought women didn't like it the first time?" She gave a slight, throaty chuckle.

"Only hotly unbridled ones like it the first time." He raised himself up on his elbows and smiled lazily down at her, patting the sides of her head. "My God, you're terrific. Thank God you're frigid. I doubt I could cope with you as a nymphomaniac."

"No other man ever set me off that way. When can we do it again?"

He shifted and sat up. "Let's go make that bed sing."

"Where'd you put my clothes?"

"Forget them. I'll drive along and take lecherous peeks at you sitting there stark naked and know I'm going to have you again." He ran his hand over his face, grinned at her, and said, "You have no idea how you affect me."

"You're entranced..."

"Right."

"By my mind?"

"Of course." He grinned as he started the truck and eased it along the track again. They really didn't drive far, but as they forded the river, Joe stopped.

"What's the matter?" she teased. "Can't you wait after all? Or are you stuck in quicksand? It would serve you right."

"Get dressed."

"What?" She was completely astonished. "What did you say?"

"Honey, be quick. Get your clothes on."

"Why?"

"Henry's at the shack."

Nine

***

Henry's pickup was big, black, and mean-looking. Henry lounged against it carelessly, his black Stetson pushed back, his faded denims soft on his male body. He was waiting for them with contented patience.

Peggy had to rebutton her jacket a second time to line up the buttons right. She clawed at her hair and covered it with the red bandanna; then she licked her fingers and smoothed her eyebrows.

As they pulled up beside Henry, he stepped away from his truck genially and strolled over. He was about to hand Peggy down from the pickup when Faraday peeked over the side of Joe's truck bed and saw Henry. He whined feebly, his eyes large and sad, as if Henry had abandoned him.

"Faraday!" Henry exclaimed. "How are you, boy? They been good to you? You look a little pale."

Peggy blinked. How could a dog look pale? He was covered with short bristly hair, for heaven's sake. She gave Faraday a disgusted look.

Henry reached up effortlessly and lifted the big dog into his arms, allowing Peggy to get herself out of the truck. Henry hugged the dog, continuing to question Faraday's state of mental and physical health as he eased him down to the ground. Faraday then sat there making a variety of sad sounds, as if replying in a negative way to all Henry's questions. Henry made sympathetic sounds in reply as he leaned over, buffeting the dog, petting him in a roughly gentle way, and the dog appeared to brace himself bravely in his weakened state.

Where was her hero dog who had challenged the bull? There was only a flabby coward in evidence. What a remarkable metamorphosis. This was a very intelligent dog.

Joe came around the back of his truck as Henry straightened up and tipped his Stetson to Peggy, who met his eyes as he asked, "How you doing?" with easy courtesy.

Before Peggy could reply, Joe said a calm, "Henry," in greeting.

Henry shook Joe's hand and laughed in real amusement for no obvious reason. Henry was bigger than Joe by an inch or two, and he was at least five years older, so his shoulders were heavier. But despite being bigger and older, and obviously a powerful man of influence and wealth, he still didn't diminish Joe. That fact interested Peggy. Especially since Joe didn't stand competitively spraddle-legged, or stretching to his tallest. He stood naturally, equally formidable.

"Tell him I'm not Francine," Peggy demanded of Henry straight out.

"Hell, Joe knows that."

"What?" she asked, frowning. She thought she had finally convinced Joe, but Henry couldn't know that. Then Joe put a possessive hand on Peggy's shoulder as she asked Henry, "How does he know?"

"What fool would leave a lone man out here with a gorgeous woman *he* loves?"

"You knew all along I wasn't..." She turned to Joe.

But it was Henry who told her, "*He* introduced *me* to Francine."

Joe smiled as Peggy turned to him.

"Then why...?" She was baffled. "Why did you keep me here? I thought *you* thought I was Francine!" She turned to Henry. "He was supposed to think I was Francine and keep me here until you came charging in here to the rescue. Why didn't you come?"

"Well now, Peggy, you know Francine. She's so obvious. I was in town all the time, right there at that hotel. I knew you weren't her when you left the elevator. I went upstairs and, sure enough, there she was. Joe had heard your signal knock and reported it to me, so I just gave the secret knock, Francine tore open the door and whispered, 'Peggy...' before she realized it was me, and then she didn't say anything else for a long time." Henry grinned like a Cheshire cat. "We're engaged."

Ignoring Joe's congratulations as he clapped Henry on his shoulder and shook his hand, Peggy said parsimoniously, "You're completely unsuited. Francine said so."

"No problem." Henry stretched lazily, then reached down to pat Faraday, who was waiting his turn for Henry's attention.

"It will never work," she pronounced.

Henry was tolerant and declined to argue.

Frustrated in that attempt, she tried to pick another argument. "Well, why didn't you come and get me? I've been here all this time."

"So?" Henry turned amused eyes to Joe. "How'd it go, Joseph Richards Mulholland? Did it work?"

"Mulholland?" Peggy asked blankly. "He said Mulholland?" She turned wide, vulnerable eyes to Joe, stepping away from him.

"Doesn't she know yet?" Henry raised his eyebrows.

"She sure as hell does now, old flapping lips."

Henry laughed.

Peggy sputtered, "You're a Mulholland? Kin to *Ziggy* Mulholland?" She gasped in speechless indignation. "Aunt Mattie's archenemy? How dare you?"

"I didn't know of any other way." Joe was reasonable as he shrugged, his eyes gentle.

"Any...other...way?" she questioned ominously.

"Now, honey, you know the Men's Club in Dallas has been trying to match us up since you came out four years ago. You've spurned all their help. We finally hit on this plan. Francine helped."

"Francine? Do you mean Francine did this to me? Led me into a trap with a Mulholland?"

"It was her idea," Henry contributed with some pride.

"All that intrigue about testing you?"

"The lure to get you to cooperate." Henry smiled.

"But you just said about the knock—"

"I was trying to see how far along Joe was with enticing you." He said over her furious sputter, "Francine knew you'd do anything to help her. And since she loves you, too, she decided to use that to get you and Joe together. You're made for each other. Francine says so."

"To merge the Matzig stock." Peggy's voice was deadly.

"Well, Matzig, Inc., *is* a tasty little company. It's just sitting there waiting for a takeover." Henry was patient. "We've been watching the stock, and we suspect someone is beginning to buy up shares. Between you and Joe, you control the company, but if one or the other of you should sell, some foreigner, from outside Texas, could get his grimy little hands on Matzig."

She lifted her chin. "So Joe has been courting my shares?"

"Not...exactly." Joe's voice held just a touch of humor.

But the core of Peggy's body had refrozen. Her face stilled, and her voice was chilly as she asked, "And you've been working on this for four years?"

"Not that first year," he admitted. "I declined the 'merger' when the opportunity came for me to study in Caracas. No sweat, though, I knew you were going to the ball with Freddy Millstone that year. Millstone hung around your neck, they tell me." He grinned cheerfully, as if she weren't slowly turning into ice.

"Then that second year you went to China. And last year you out-and-out declined to attend. You told the Men's Club in a polite little note that you'd be embarrassed to attend their frolic—where did you find that word?—since you would be so much older than the other girls...."

"Women," she snapped.

"Ah, yes. You did indeed say women," Joe agreed.

"You...saw my note?"

"And took one hell of a ribbing over it. They even suggested you were avoiding me."

"I was. I *am,* Mr. Mulholland." She turned with great dignity to Henry. "Will you please take me home? I've had enough."

Henry's look of being highly entertained slipped, and he frowned a little. "Do you really want to leave Joe?"

"Now," she replied with emphasis.

"Honey—" Joe reached out a placating hand.

"Don't you touch me! You may say my...audition was a failure."

"Now, wait a minute."

Henry put in, "Having a little trouble, Joe?"

"Nothing I can't handle."

"Please," she said commandingly to Henry. "Shall we go?"

"Sorry, Joe." Henry dug his keys from his pocket. "It was worth the try."

She turned away from the two men and walked with stiff, frozen pride toward Henry's pickup. Joe strode after her, reached out, and took her arm in his hard hand. "Now, just a minute, Peggy."

She swung around. "Peggy? Now you call me Peggy? Just because I'm a major shareholder in Matzig, Inc.?"

"I don't care about the damn stock! Now, look here, Peggy—"

"You may refer to me as Miss Dillon. I'm going to sue you for unlawful detention, womannapping, and holding me against my will. Let go of me!"

"I know a good lawyer," Henry told her helpfully.

"Henry..." Joe's tone was a stern warning.

"Sorry."

"I *said* let go of me!" Peggy jerked her arm and then began to struggle seriously. Joe held her effortlessly, still trying to get her to listen, but suddenly Faraday was there beside them—and he growled at Joe!

Joe looked down at the dog and asked indignantly, "Are you growling at me?"

The dog looked uncertain. But Peggy again tried to get loose from Joe, and again Faraday growled.

That offended Joe, and he stopped and frowned at Faraday, saying, "I'm the guy who gave you more syrup on your pancakes!"

Henry came alert. "You gave Faraday...pancakes?"

"With syrup!" Peggy tattled. "Henry, will you sell Faraday to me?"

"Why?" Obviously that surprised even Henry.

"He protects me from unwanted males—like Joe, and the bull this morning when I—"

"Bull?" Henry grew very still, and his voice was like a rumble of thunder. "What...bull?"

"This morning when I finally escaped. Faraday was magnificent! I was terrified—"

"You put Faraday in danger?" Henry's eyes flashed with temper.

"Don't you speak to her that way." Joe shot a threatening look at Henry.

"You do," Henry pointed out.

"*I* can." Joe's free hand lifted, and although his thumb touched his own chest, it was in very real challenge to Henry. Not only dogs could go back to nature; the veneer of civilization was extremely thin on men, too.

"You gave Faraday pancakes?" Henry repeated, as if to clarify causes.

"And chili." With some satisfaction Peggy threw the additional charge in the hopper.

"Chili?" Henry rocked back on his bootheels. "Pancakes and chili? What chili? *My* chili? How could you do that to Faraday? It isn't fit for most *people*, much less Faraday's delicate innards. How could you do that to my dog?'' He was becoming hostile.

"Henry," warned Joe, "I'm in no mood, right now, to discuss that damned, spoiled dog of yours who was once my friend. You can take your dog and—"

The two men moved belligerently forward, so Peggy said coldly, "I am waiting to leave."

Henry looked at her as if he had lost track of her and she had appeared out of nowhere, while Joe's grip on her arm tightened. Joe said, "No."

Faraday growled, and Henry finally realized how out-of-hand the situation was and said to Joe, "It's best to let her go. She looks as if she's been through a lot, and any decision she'd make now might be influenced by her feelings of animosity caused by living rather crudely, for a woman, without a good hot tub and clean clothes. Francine said Peggy hated the purple suit. It looked terrific on Francine, but she's a stronger personality."

"It looks good on Peggy," Joe ground out.

"Maybe you need a hot tub, too," Henry observed. "Obviously you both need a little time apart. Come on, Peggy, I'll take you home. And Joe, you can get in touch in a day or so." Crooning comfortingly, Henry lifted his dog into the back of his pickup, leaving Peggy to pry Joe's fingers from her arm.

Joe hadn't realized how tightly he had been holding her and was ashamed when he saw the white marks his fingers left on her arm. He knew she would be bruised. He looked at her, and as beautiful as she was, he saw that her nose was sunburned, her hair was in clumps, and she was still wearing that purple suit—which was now good only for throwing away. Actually she looked gorgeous, fragile but ill-used, and he felt like a rat. "Peggy..." But how could he talk to her there?

She gave him a killing look that was full of hurt, then she got into the truck and slid over against the far door. Joe was appalled at this turn of events. Had he lost her? Surely not. Then he reached into his shirt pocket and handed her the toothbrush he had bought for her in town that morning, and he said very seriously, "I got this for you."

She automatically put her hand out to take it, but her eyes didn't register what she was receiving. She looked at Joe seriously as Henry clapped him on the shoulder and said, "Keep in touch," before he slid into the driver's side.

Henry was so big that he made the pickup look as if it were a toy truck. He put the key in the ignition, switched it on, and then the motor roared and the truck moved.

Henry swung the truck in a slow, wide, easy circle, and Joe turned, following it with his eyes. Following Peggy with his eyes. And as the truck went on down the track, she watched him in the side mirror on her door as he grew smaller and smaller. Finally she turned sideways; from the corner of her eyes she could still see him, standing there, watching Henry's truck disappear.

She was leaving him. Leaving him back there where she had lived with him for four days. Had it only been four days? It seemed like a lifetime.

How could a Mulholland be so charming? So sweet? So insidiously seductive? He had lured her to surrender.

She looked down and saw the toothbrush. Tears welled in her eyes and slipped down her cheeks. She held it in her palm as if it were a precious gem. He had gone into town to buy her a toothbrush. He had done that for her.

He had known all along that she wasn't Francine. They had contrived to put her out there alone with Joe to allow time and propinquity to work on them, to make her aware of him, to encourage her into a relationship. He had known. He had known all along that she wasn't Francine.

He had tricked her. She had gone along with it all, thinking she was being so clever, and it had all been an elaborate ruse because she was a major shareholder in Great Aunt Mattie's business. It had all been done for money.

Well, not necessarily just for money. They didn't want her shares or the stock or the income. Although they didn't want her to sell, the real purpose had been to get her and Joe together. And behind it all was the Dallas Men's Club which had been matching fortunes and fortune's children for generations.

Why risk having money and companies go to strangers? Probably into inept hands, where the fortunes would be dissipated, the companies ruined. Why not guide the children into marriages that not only were suitable, but which would preserve fortunes in hands that would continue to use the money well?

But why had the club ever been so rash as to try to match up Mattie and Ziggy's great niece and nephew? How incredible! What foolish men to fly in the face of the turbulent animosity that had been engendered in the founders of Matzig, Inc., and try to couple their young kin. It did make one wonder how many other unsuitable, careless tries had been made, how many couples had married who should never have been paired.

Joe had said his second name was Richards, and she had just assumed it was his last name. In all her growing-up years, with her daddy in the army and so seldom visiting Texas for any length of time, she had never met Joe Mulholland.

It was odd that Aunt Mattie was the only one who despised the Mulhollands. Everyone else appeared to like and even to *trust* them. Not Aunt Mattie. She had been vitriolic about Ziggy Mulholland...and Joe was one of *them*.

It *had* been "Mulholland" that Ramon had said! And Joe— old smooth-tongued Joe—had said, "I didn't hear it." No. He hadn't yet gotten her to commit herself to him and couldn't risk her knowing his name. Another tricky Mulholland.

He was so clever. So sweet and funny. So beautifully made. And he had bought her a toothbrush. He had gone into town and bought her a toothbrush!

She turned tear-filled eyes to Henry and said in a shaky, vulnerable voice, "He bought me this toothbrush." And she lifted her hand to show him the precious thing.

Henry was driving very slowly because of the roughness of the track and for Faraday's comfort, so he turned surprised eyes to Peggy. He saw her forlorn expression, and the tears, and asked, "Huh?"

"He went into town this morning and he bought me a toothbrush."

"Obviously you're hooked on toothbrushes?" Henry puzzled over that. "It never occurred to me to buy Francine a *toothbrush*. This some kinky new twist?"

"I told him I was going to carry a toothbrush and a change of underwear with me in my purse from now on. My teeth were turning green with mold, and he made me a toothbrush from a twig. It worked quite well. He's very clever." She gulped back a sob.

Henry gave her a cautiously curious look and was silent.

"And the moccasins." Peggy turned her foot to show him the crudely remodeled moccasins.

"That elk-hide? I have some elk-hide moccasins at the... Are those...*my* elk-hide moccasins? Say no," Henry urged anxiously.

"As a matter of fact, they could be. Joe found them on top of the cupboard...."

Henry gave a heartfelt groan, and Faraday barked inquiringly, so Henry had to say, "It's okay, boy." But he added under his breath in real torment, "My elk-hide moccasins." It was obvious he was suffering.

By then they had come to the stream where Peggy had sunk Francine's car into the quicksand. Peggy sat forward as she recognized the spot—but the car was gone! She gasped, "Someone has stolen Francine's car!"

"Oh, no," he said calmly. "We got it out that same afternoon. You know Francine can't survive without her car. I'm still astounded that she allowed you to take it. She must trust you."

"Yes," Peggy said sadly. "She still can. But she betrayed me."

"She loves you."

"Loving isn't trusting. I'll never trust her again," she declared with great disillusion.

"Now, Peggy, you'll break her heart. I can't allow that."

"I won't make a point of telling her I no longer trust her. I just won't. How could she have done this to me? And you, Henry, you say you're engaged to Francine?

"You're fickle and a womanizer and a workaholic. How can you trap Francine into marriage? You've courted her and paid attention to her and she thinks that's how it'll go on, but you'll lose interest in her and not see her, and she'll feel unhappy and abandoned. You can't marry her. You'd be kinder to give her up."

"Don't worry about us. We've got it all worked out," Henry assured her. "I really do love her. She's going to be all right. I'll take good care of her. You don't have to worry about any of it. And, Peggy, you know Francine wouldn't do a thing to harm you. Joe's a good man. Honorable, true, a solid citizen. You couldn't find any man to match him, other than me, and I'm taken."

They drove in silence toward San Antonio. Peggy was wrung out, so she tended to be weepy. At the outskirts of town Henry asked, "Home? Or your place?"

If she went home her mother would more than likely find the whole affair very amusing. Her mother was a little strange. Her place was another of Mattie's gifts. A refuge. It was now declared a historical treasure under the protection of the U.S. But it was hers to cherish as long as she lived, and she could hand it down to "...the issue of (her) body." When there was no issue, the government would supervise the selling to a private citizen who would care for it properly. She told Henry, "My place."

It was stucco. The walls were two feet thick and the floors were all red clay tile. There were fireplaces in the corners of all the small rooms, and the house was as cool as a kind hand in the summer and as warm as toast in winter. She would go there and lick her emotional wounds. "My place," she repeated. "I need to be alone."

"I'll tell Francine you're back."

"No, I'll call her. I'm really tired. I want to sleep."

"Well, how about supper with us tonight?"

"I'll probably go home for supper," she said evasively.

They didn't speak again until he walked her to her door. Her place was in the center of the city on the San Antonio River. He said, "Give Joe a chance."

"Thanks for bringing me home."

"See him."

"Tell Francine I'll be in touch."

"At least talk to him on the phone, Peggy. He's a good man."

"If you ever want to sell Faraday, give me first refusal."

"You're a stubborn woman."

"I'm a major shareholder. Never forget that."

"*You* should forget it. Joe wants nothing to do with your stock. He's not interested in your shares."

"Do you realize I have a rather impressive portfolio? I'm a good catch. Aunt Mattie saw to it that I'd be independent and that I could have the choice of how I want to run my life."

"I hope dear old Matilda is roasting to a turn."

"How rude you are."

"No. You've edged me out with your treatment of Joe."

"*Him?* He captured me, he kept me prisoner, he—"

"He didn't harm you. He went to great lengths to assure your safety out there."

"From drug runners and illegal aliens?" What about from Joe himself?

"They're very secretive. They generally stay away from people. I'm talking about saddle tramps, wandering roughnecks."

"Protecting Matzig's principal stockholder."

"He doesn't need your paltry little bit of accumulated stocks—or bonds—or property. You could keep it all for pin money. You have no conception of how wealthy he is or the ramifications of his influence. And he's still a young man.

"If Joe was as poor as a country church mouse, he'd still be worth ten of any other man, except me, and you'd be lucky to hand over every penny you have to him, if that's what it took to have him. You need to really look at the man."

She gestured with an impatient hand.

"Work at it." He put a friendly hand briefly on her shoulder and patted it just a bit more gently than he buffeted Faraday. "Take care of yourself. We'll be around." He touched the brim of his Stetson and strode off to his truck, where he lifted a lax Faraday from the back of the truck into the cab. The dog began whining in a marvelous variety of tones. Henry said, "Is that right?" And Peggy thought, now Henry has to deal with Faraday's complaints.

As she closed and locked her front door behind herself, Peggy pensively turned off her doorbell. She went over to the phone, ignored the messages on her machine, and called her parents. The housekeeper answered. Peggy said, "I'm at my place. I'm going to take a nap and I'll call later."

The housekeeper was mumbling about running all over the state and doing God only knew what all, when Peggy again said, "I'll call later," and eased the phone back on the hook.

Peggy thought that there she had been, with that threateningly attractive man, and her parents were out running around without one thought turned her way. There she'd been with that stupid dog, trudging across the burning sands, through forests of mesquite and cactus, attacked by a bull, and they had gone their busy way. No one really cared about her.

She looked forlornly around at the beautiful things that Aunt Mattie had collected in that elegant, treasured house, and she would have traded it all to get back to that shack. She disconnected the phone, leaking some tears, but she knew the tears were only because she was so strung out emotionally and so bone-tired.

In the mirrored bathroom, hung with gauzy drapes, she considered that her prim aunt must have had the soul of a harlot. She filled the green and aqua tiled bath, the water spouting from the mouth of a graceful fish. She tipped a handful of bath oil into the foaming water to see if she could salvage her parched skin which had barely been saved from the buzzards.

While the tub filled, she went into her kitchen, took off that stupid, ugly, purple suit and dropped it into the wastebasket with shuddering revulsion and a great deal of satisfaction.

She stalked back to the bathroom and lowered her weary, dried-out body into the hot, filling tub, and slid down as she closed her eyes at the pleasure of it.

The water crept up over her body in a lovely, sensuous way, and she wished Joe was...there? A Mulholland? There in the tub and making love to her? Well, it was just that this bath was a whole world away from the baths at the shack. This was how a bath should be.

But it had been lovely there, too. That freezing pond...and he had claimed it de-sexed him! What an impossible idea that was! And he had stood there so unself-conscious, so magnificently male, so interested in her shares of Matzig, Inc.

But he had made love to her so beautifully, and he had bought her the toothbrush. She rose from the bath, dripped into her bedroom, got the toothbrush from her purse and went back into the bath to hold it. It was purple.

She opened the plastic case and slid the toothbrush out of its holder and dreamily ran her finger over the bristles. They were like his morning beard. Not too stiff, not too soft, just right.

He had held her sleepy body against his hard length, and he had kissed her so wonderfully, so thrillingly, and nudged his whiskers into the side of her throat.... On its own her body moved in the hot oily water, and she sighed.

What would it be like if he were there with her now in that tub-for-two with its warm caressing waters, their bodies slippery, sliding together...his hard hands sliding down her, moving on her, searching her out?

His intentions had been honorable. It surprised her to admit that. He hadn't taken her out there to use her and toss her aside. He was an honorable man.

It was then that she realized the reason he hadn't taken her sooner was that he'd had no protection for her. That was why he had gone into town, not just to buy her that toothbrush. That was why, when they left the Gonzaleses' house, he had told her he was going to make love to her for a week. He had been thoughtful enough to want to protect her.

And at the shack, at that crucial time, there was Henry. After not showing up for four days, why did Henry have to choose that particular time to arrive? He could have waited another couple of days. Then Joe would have had the time to...make love to her enough to last her for the rest of her life.

She could never marry a Mulholland. Marry Great Aunt Mattie's archenemy's kin? Mattie would probably haunt her for the rest of her days and hound her through eternity.

But Joe might be worth that threat. With all the reading material available about sex and how to go about it, none of it substituted for the real thing. Now she knew what it was like.

Before Joe, she had certainly had her share of opportunities to find out how it was. Men were eager to initiate any reasonably curious woman, but she had never wanted to. It was too personal.

Making love was not something one did casually. Simple curiosity or wanting wasn't a good enough excuse to indulge in experimentation. For it to be right and fulfilling, it had to be with a man she cared enough about to want him forever. It had to be more than just sex. It had to be making love. It had to be with...Joe.

She was a one-man woman. She faced that probability. And Joe was that man. How could she love a man, and sleep with him, and make love with him, when he wasn't really interested in *her* but in her shares of stocks? Henry had admitted that the Men's Club had taken that into consideration in pairing them off.

But Joe had said it wasn't her stock that he'd been working on. And Henry said Joe had more money and more interests than anyone could ever know. Was it possible that Joe wanted her? That of all the women available to him, Joe had chosen her? That was too astonishing. Why would he want her? If he'd known all along that she wasn't Francine, what besides the stock was the reason he would kidnap her and hold her there at the shack?

Who was right? Great Aunt Mattie? "Men are wicked and tricky." That was what she'd said. "Never trust a man. Be independent. I'll see to it you have the means. You don't need a man. You can buy a parrot to cuss at you, a dog to growl at you, and a cat to stay out all night.''

Aunt Mattie had never married. She had lived a busy, carefree, single life. And the man she had cursed and railed at the most was Sigfried Mulholland. What a combination of names. A German mother and an Irish father. Ziggy. He must have been an ogre. He had sure cured Aunt Mattie of all men. To *think* they had ever been civil enough for long enough to have created Matzig, Inc. It was unbelievable.

If Aunt Mattie hadn't met Ziggy so early in her life, would she have married? Would she have found men less abrasive, less distasteful? What if she had met someone like…Joe? Would he have melted Mattie's solidly frozen core as Joe had hers?

From ice to lava, that's what Joe had done to her. How had her delicate, sensitive tissue survived? He had melted her down and enflamed her to molten heat. A heat of hunger and longing and desire. All for her shares of Matzig, Inc.

What did it matter if foreigners from outside Texas owned Matzig, Inc.? What if someone from Pennsylvania or Montana or Florida should buy her stock? Texans just might be prejudiced. Was she so open-minded because she was a halfbreed? Part Hoosier?

She could sell the stock and wait and see what Joe would do then. Would he continue to be interested in her? If she sold her stock, Great Aunt Mattie would come down from her particular cloud, lay her harp aside in her formal, clearing-things-out-of-the-way manner, and she would say to her, ''Margaret, you are a ninny. I gave you that stock so you could be independent. You are letting emotional involvement—sex—sway you into doing something purely asinine. You're smarter than that. Keep your independence. Don't sign any papers.

''Get Bertie to draw up an unbreakable premarital agreement if you should lose your head over that man and stupidly contemplate handing your life and independence over to him.''

Bertie was no longer in this vale of sin and tears. He had withered away rather rapidly just after Mattie had left this world of stocks and bonds. But a prenuptial agreement wasn't a bad idea. It would be interesting to see how...how *any* man would view one. Would a man sign away control of his intended's fortune?

It would take a strong, self-confident man to allow money and control to remain in a woman's hands. It would be a very telling test to confront a man with such an agreement and witness his reaction.

Ten

After her hot bath, with her muscles turned to mush, Peggy drooped into the bedroom and slid naked between the pink satin sheets on her perfect, soundless, civilized bed, and she went instantly to sleep. However, it wasn't a restful, soothing nap. She dreamed.

She presented Joe with a prenuptial agreement. He was seated meekly at a table with his hands folded. The meekness caused her to frown suspiciously, even in her sleep. She sailed the document onto the table and stood, her feet firmly placed, her hands on her hips, her nose in the air. Would he sign?

"Darling..." His low voice floated seductively through the air, insidiously unwomaning her. "Don't you trust me?"

His eyes melted her insides, but she replied, "It's a formality."

He chided, "You don't want to be burdened with all that nasty old business. Let me take care of you and your stocks and bonds." And he smiled in the sly, teasing way of a man who knew he would have his way with her. And he would.

"What's this?" he asked in another dream, taking up the document as he rose from the table to tower over her. "Why, honey, you needn't worry your pretty little head with anything like this." He pitched the paper toward the wastebasket and didn't even need to watch to see if it floated in. He just reached for her as he went on, "Come here, woman, and please me." That was what he would say, and that was what she would do. She knew it.

The variations of his not signing the prenuptial agreement went on and on, but he never signed one of them. Not one.

Aunt Mattie's disembodied but unmistakable voice commented more than once, "See? I told you."

After that Peggy's dreams changed and she tossed and turned and became entangled in the satin sheets which caressed her body and slid along her skin just like Joe's hands. She awoke more tired than when she lay down, and she was very disturbed and unhappy.

She crawled out of bed, took a cold shower, pulled on shorts and a top, and padded barefooted across the cool clay tiles to the kitchen, knowing she should eat something. She made a peanut butter sandwich with lettuce and tomato slices and drank a glass of milk.

She listened to her phone recorder's taped messages. There were several bubbly ones from Francine, and a merry one from her mother telling her to call home when she returned from her "little adventure"—and for some reason her mother laughed. Several friends said to call back. Then there was Joe. The last five were from Joe.

Two were from the pay phone out on the highway, with the sounds of additional coins dropping into the slot. He gave his phone number and said he would be there, or he would leave the phone number wherever he would be. He needed to talk to her.

Peggy listened to his voice and tried to harden her heart. Why couldn't he have a thin, squeaky voice?

Restless, she paced around the house; then, before dark, she went out to pace along the river walk. Back home again, she went into the kitchen and stood there eyeing the wastebasket. Slowly she went over, lifted the wicker lid, and looked down at the crumpled purple suit lying discarded inside.

She almost put the lid back on, but then she laid it aside and reached in to retrieve the ghastly purple mess. She took it out, held it up and surveyed it with hazy, unclear eyes; then she held it against her, closed her eyes, hugged it, and wept.

She took that awful suit to her bedroom and laid it on her bed, smoothing it out. Joe had held that suit. When he had held her, he had held that suit, and he had unbuttoned the buttons as he laid her back....

Miserable, she folded the suit with gentle hands, rolled the crudely altered moccasins inside, then put the bundle into the bottom of a plastic storage bag in her closet. She didn't actually sort out why in the world she had rescued that poisonously hateful purple suit, but she knew all the same.

Still with the recorder on the phone, with the lights out in the apartment, she watched the day close down—and the horizon rise—before she put on her nightgown, drank a glass of warm milk, and went back to bed.

It was strange to sleep alone. The bed was so big. She went over in her mind every word and gesture of Joe's. Every smile was replayed, and every one showed his chipped tooth. Gradually she slipped into sleep.

It was astonishing to have a choice of clothing the next morning. And shoes! But her elation was brief. She was alone. Where had Joe slept last night? Had he missed her? She even missed Faraday! The very thought of her missing Faraday made her smile, but the smile was pale and wan.

She became gloomy as she wished herself back in the shack— with Joe. Not just *a* Joe, but with Joe Mulholland.

She listened to the phone tapes, and the call she returned was to her mother, who chattered, "How are you, child? How was your little holiday? Did you see anyone...interesting?" And again she laughed. How strange.

Why had her mother asked if she'd seen anyone "interest ing"? Well, of course, she *always* asked that question. Bein the only daughter of an instinctively avid matchmaker had no been at all easy for Peggy. Eventually she would have to marr just to escape her mother's matrimonial attentions. Eithe marry or enter a convent.

In microseconds Peggy considered the list of males he mother had coaxed her into dating—from those against whom she'd had to defend herself tooth and nail to those who had sa like dead lumps. Zeros, every one.

Of each current choice her mother would say, "But darling he's such a *nice* young man, and his mother would be such *perfect mother-in-law*!" Or she would say, "He's an only child and you have to be kind to only children." Peggy had found— firsthand—that only children are just like everyone else.

Freddy Millstone was one candidate her mother was stil pushing. His mother was Annabelle Dillon's best friend an would be the "ideal" mother-in-law. But Freddy was like un seasoned, refried beans—bland and a little gassy.

Peggy's attention returned to her mother, who was still rat tling on about the family, and then Mrs. Dillon said, "...an don't forget the cocktail party for the gallery—day after to morrow! Besides everyone else, all the family will be there You're committed for five hundred—"

"Dollars? Mother, I can't afford all your little fund raisers."

Her mother disagreed, "Besides Matzig, Inc. you have Aun Mattie's stocks and bonds, and no commitments, and you ca easily help out."

"But I would like to choose my own ways of 'helping out and how much I give. You're always telling me how to spen my money."

"It's a good cause, darling. Fabian is so fragile; he need support."

"He's dreadful."

"Well, I must admit I'm relieved you're not interested in him romantically."

Peggy snorted.

"His mother is *strange*. She's so domineering; she'd try to run your life for you. She'd be a terrible mother-in-law!"

"No chance," Peggy assured her own domineering mother. "All he can do is look like an abused bloodhound and kiss hands. I've had dogs do it neater."

"You have no soul."

"Fabian obviously told you that you have soul?"

"And sensitivity."

"Is Daddy going?"

"Of course. He stands and gnashes his teeth at Fabian and tests out the capability of his blood pressure pills."

Peggy laughed. "That's...sensitivity? Making Daddy gnash his teeth?"

"Awareness. I have that, too."

"I'm amazed Daddy puts up with you."

"He gets to take me home." Her mother's voice went low and sexy and made Peggy laugh again. "Day after tomorrow," Mrs. Dillon reminded her daughter. "*Every*one will be there. And you, too, Margaret; you be there."

"You do try one's soul."

"It's excellent for your character."

That day Peggy received one red rose, and later one chocolate-covered cherry in a silver box with an enameled top. The next day a tattered book of Elizabeth Barrett Browning's poems was delivered to her door, and then a tiny slipper on a chain so fragile that the slipper appeared to float on her chest.

There was no name on any of the cards. Just "With all my love." How confident of him! He thought she would know exactly who had sent her such charming gifts.

How clever he was to think of a slipper after keeping her barefooted for three days. It was platinum. Much too expensive to keep. However, since she couldn't possibly find the time that day to return it, she could wear it for a while.

She carried the rose around, and her eyes and nose dripped because she had rose fever. She mooned over the flower and

made little whimpering sounds that should have horrified her
to her very backbone. Why did Joe have to be a Mulholland!

The flower drooped, very similarly to her own attitude, and
it began to turn dark as it died. She put it between wax paper
and pressed it under her Bible which had been willed to her by
a lady to whom Peggy had given an electric wheelchair. The
Bible was in German, and the spidery writing which listed people and the birth and death dates was faded into oblivion.

If Peggy had taken German instead of French she could have
read the passages and found solace for her torn life. The passages would say that any woman who would get tangled up with
Joseph Mulholland deserved all the torment she received—and
to quit whining about it.

She went through her clothes and was again amazed at how
many there were. She had never realized the variety she pos-
sessed. Actually, she had more than she needed. But she had
nothing at all to wear the next evening at the gallery.

Her mother had put her down for a five-hundred-dollar do-
nation! She would be listed as a Patron in gold-colored letter-
ing on the program, and her name would then go on every
single charity hit-list in all of Texas, and out to other states and
foreign countries. Her mail would drive her mad, with every
letter beginning "Give..." How could her mother have done
this to her?

Peggy sighed as she flicked through the choices. She could
wear the remnants of the poisonously purple suit. Would people think the five hundred was a mistake and cross her off their
lists? No, they would just think she was eccentric, like Howard
Hughes.

She ended up wearing a resale gown from the Junior League
Boutique. It was a little strange. The Leaguer who had been
caught contributing it had never had the courage to wear it, and
no one, browsing through, had given it anything but a startled
glance. However, one dull day when Peggy had been assigned
to work there she had found it fit her perfectly. Her friends, and
the contributor, would occasionally ask, "When are you going
to wear it? You've chickened out, right?"

The outfit was wildly patterned in pink and orange on a slip top attached to wide pajama pants. Wearing it, she couldn't drink anything, because too many hidden hooks had to be undone in order to get it down to go to the bathroom.

She put it on, stood in front of the full-length mirror, and surveyed herself. She looked as if the five hundred contribution had been a typo and anyone asking her for money was wasting the stationery and stamp.

She spent an anguished night, dreaming that Joe had been adopted and wasn't actually a Mulholland, but she knew that wasn't so, and that he was lost to her forever. But life must go on.

So the next evening she showed up at the gallery with her hair on top of her head and an orange organza butterfly with a seven-inch wing-span sitting on top of her hair. The air current as she walked caused the butterfly's wings to move minutely, as if it were resting contentedly there.

But as weird as she looked, she was completely eclipsed by Fabian's show. She looked ordinary, in comparison. In fact, she looked like an easy mark, but her mother had saved her by listing her five hundred dollar contribution as given by "An Art Lover."

Peggy read that, then looked unbelievingly around the packed gallery walls—squinting her eyes a little when confronted by the onslaught of color. Then she saw Francine approaching through the noisy mob that cheerfully filled the gallery.

"Why didn't you return my calls?" her "twin" scolded.

Peggy stiffened at being confronted by her betrayer, who had deliberately thrown her into isolation with a Mulholland. Her lips tightened. Francine was in a floating chiffon of a creamy yellow tint that looked gorgeously restful in that exotic mishmash. "Oh, yes. Francine," Peggy said coolly, as if she'd only just placed the other woman's identity. "How have you been?"

"Did you have a delicious...holiday?" Francine's eyes sparkled in a very naughty way, and her smile was equally wicked, and knowing.

"I don't care to discuss it with you," Peggy replied and turned away.

Francine reached out and stopped her and, with the crowd pressing around, Peggy was briefly trapped. Francine frowned at her. "You're immune to Joe, *too*?"

"Joe?" Peggy inquired, as if searching her mind to place him. "Oh. You must mean Joseph...Mulholland?"

"Are you implying that after four days with *Joe* you're still a virgin?"

Whose business was it if she was or wasn't? "Excuse me, Francine, I have to find my dad." She slid her way through the crowd, leaving Francine staring after her.

Peggy found her brothers one by one, and they all managed to tell her that Joe Mulholland had always been a guy they liked. He was a good sport, open-minded, smart, flexible, athletic, good company, and could play a piano like no one else.

Yeah. The piano probably started humming as soon as he sat down nearby. Just like a woman would. Were pianos male? Or were they female, like ships?

Then she came on Ramon and Teresa Gonzales! Peggy smiled and said, "Hello," enunciating carefully. She couldn't do too much to mispronounce hello, and the word was recognized in many countries.

Teresa replied, "You look marvelous! The bull got out again that afternoon, and Ramon sold it to Joe! He said something about bronzing it! Can you imagine? Why would Joe want to bronze a bull?"

"You speak...?" Peggy stood there with her mouth open.

"English?" Teresa laughed. "Of course. Our ancestors were here even before the Spanish, and we adapt to other languages reasonably well. I teach English at the collective high school near our summer place and—"

"Summer place? Then..."

"And I should tell you that my teeth are safe." Teresa grinned in delight. "This is Ramon's and my first baby. The others are children of sisters and brothers who were spending the day with us so the cousins could get to know each other."

"Why did you pretend to speak only Spanish?"

It was Ramon who replied; Teresa only gave a big grin. He said, "Joe explained your quarrel. He said he needed time with you to smooth things over, and he asked us to please speak only Spanish because then you would think you were unable to ask us for help. I knew he'd never hurt you."

"He's a Mulholland."

Ramon shrugged at that and agreed. "All his very life."

They didn't even have accents! The Gonzaleses spoke just like everyone else. The crowd eddied and Peggy, embarrassed, allowed herself to shift away from them, lifting a hand and mouthing an "I'll be in touch."

It wasn't a putoff; Peggy would contact Teresa. She needed to know someone who could tolerate the kind of birth-control lecture she had given Teresa and had refrained from replying when she easily could have!

Just then one of the roadblockers came along and spoke to Ramon and Teresa before he came on past Peggy. So the road-blockers had known the Gonzaleses all along. The road-blocker said, "Hi, Peggy. How'd it go?" And he chuckled!

"You know that I'm not Francine?"

"Margaret Indiana Dillon, just like on your driver's license." He grinned amicably.

"If you know, you're an accessory!"

"Now, Peggy, you know I'm not going to admit to that. You know Joe's harmless."

Harmless? Joe?

And there over her cousin Tom's shoulder was Joe! What was *he* doing there? He grinned, so full of himself that she exclaimed, "You!" Her eyes grew enormous. And there she was in that god-awful outfit.

"My God!" he replied in delight. "Instant recognition! How astonishing!" He was wearing a tux, and he looked magnificent.

Parsimoniously, she replied, "Of course I recognize you. I spent four days studying you so the FBI wouldn't have any trouble finding you once I escaped from you."

He ignored her bristling words and said, "I wasn't sure— these last two days—that I hadn't dreamed you." His eyes were tender on her despite the intervening heads and shoulders. "You do look just lovely."

She turned her head away as if she were hunting for someone, but her eyes couldn't focus on anything. Lovely? He thought she looked lovely? Well, of course, he had only seen her in that purple suit and...naked. But lovely? In that orange-and-pink whatever with a butterfly on top of her head? He had strange taste.

Joe reached past everyone else and took her arm. "Would you excuse me?" he asked the heads and shoulders.

"Go away!" Peggy snapped, but she didn't take her arm from his hand.

"I don't think she wants to go along." Her cousin Tom frowned.

"You know how women are...well, hello there, Tom. How you been?"

"Joe? I didn't recognize you all cleaned up."

"Women are a pain, coming to these things, and it was the only way I could track Peggy down."

"Yeah," Tom agreed, then he told Peggy, "Go along." And he moved so Joe could tug her past him. "See what Joe wants," Tom advised her cheerfully.

"I *know* what he wants," she told her cousin through her teeth.

"Now, that's a blessing." And Joe grinned, very amused.

"What about what *I* want?" she asked, her eyes solemn.

"I'm *trying* to sort you out, so's you'll know."

"Sort me out?"

Despite the crowd, he took her into his arms and held her as he sighed, "Oh. Now this *is* nice." His shoulders curled forward and he pulled her into his body.

And her silly body—all on its own—agreed. To be close to him again! She pretended that the man in back of her in the crush was pressing her even closer. "Sorry," she said insincerely as she flicked her eyelashes up and sneaked a peek at him.

"Be my guest." He held her even tighter, and his strong arms squeezed the air from her lungs. His hard hands resisted crushing her, but moved on her back and relished the feel of her. "Is your arm okay, honey? I worried I'd hurt you." He tried to see where he'd held her arm too tightly when she had left him with Henry. "Is it okay?"

She had covered the darkened spot with makeup. "I gave your finerprints to the FBI," she told him saucily, her eyes on his black tie, her hands against his chest. He was there. She glanced up.

He smiled into her eyes; then his glance went on down to her obviously feminine chest and he said gruffly, "So you got my gifts?"

And she realized she was still wearing the little platinum slipper. Her mind groped in all directions, and her tongue came up with, "I've learned to bring extra shoes with me or go bare-footed." She had instructed her tongue to sound sarcastic, but the words had come out breathless and a bit flirtatious. Probably because he was holding her so tightly that she didn't have enough air.

Only Joe noticed when the crowd shifted and there was enough space behind Peggy that she could have moved back, away from him, but she didn't. He didn't mention it, and anyway his arms held her tightly to him, and her body was relaxed and softly unresisting.

"Want some champagne?" In the babble of chatter and laughter he said it right against her ear. His head was tilted a little sideways to avoid disturbing the butterfly, and he took advantage of his mouth being right there and breathed gently in her ear.

She looked up at him, her pupils enormously dilated, and her lips solemnly formed the words, "I can't drink anything," having in mind the difficulty of getting her weird outfit undone.

"Me either. Just being near you makes me drunk." He hugged her closer.

If she got any closer to him, they would be melded together. That caused her memory to race back to her other moments of...closeness with Joe. She went boneless and dizzy. Then he kissed her. It was a hot, seriously intent kiss.

When he slowly raised his head from hers, her eyelids were heavy, her lips had to stay parted for her to breathe, and her hands fluttered like butterfly wings in a mesmerized manner.

She grasped at protective straws. "My parents..."

"Lovely people," he murmured. "We'll be quite compatible."

"They don't know about you," she told him earnestly.

"Oh, yes. I sent them a message as soon as I stole you."

She lazily twisted an obstinately straight lock of his hair around her finger. His daughters would all have to have permanents, she thought musingly, but they would have his eyelashes in compensation.

His breath was very hot alongside her head and shoulder. "The minute I laid eyes on you, I knew you were mine. I agreed to Francine's plan because I couldn't think of any other way, and opportunity knocks only once."

"You knew who I was all along."

"Ummmmhmmmm. But it seemed the smartest thing was just to play along and pretend you were Francine and all. To see if you really were as darling as you appeared to be."

"I can't believe you went to all that trouble."

"I'd go to the moon for you." His voice was a husky groan, and his hands moved on her back as if they longed to do a whole lot more.

She smiled tenderly up at him. "What sort of message did you send my parents? Did you say, 'I've stolen Peggy for carnal purposes'?"

"Actually, I didn't know whether I'd make a go of it with you. I just told them you were visiting a very good friend."

"Friend?"

"That was before I'd slept with you that first night." He moved his arms to hug her again very, very nicely. "Then I went up yesterday to see them and explained how it is between us."

"Exactly how *do* you think it is? Between us?"

"I confessed to your father that I'd compromised you unsalvageably, and I'd probably have to marry you. I'd accepted that as my duty, but I needed his permission to convince you."

"Your...duty?"

He nodded with a long-suffering sigh. "With maybe just a bit of hanky-panky tucked in here and there—now and then?" His quick grin revealed his chipped tooth.

"Hmmm. What did they say?" One forefinger traced the rim of his ear.

"They were some surprised you'd been...misplaced. Your mother laughed."

"She would."

"But your dad was cautious."

"He thought you wanted a reward? A dowry?"

"No. I think he was weighing me up. I suspect he was trying to judge how much he could get out of me. You know how thorough the army is and how they cling to traditions. He was more than likely taught bead-trading at West Point from the same book that got us New York for twenty-four dollars. And he thought he could get a good deal out of me."

"*From* you?"

"For me taking you off his hands." Joe again exposed the chip. "He's army, and the army never gives anything up willingly."

"You beast." Her tone was mild and indulgent.

"After I convinced them I really wanted you, your mother wanted to come watch me convince you."

Peggy smiled fondly and slowly shook her head, saying again, "She would."

"But your daddy told her that you hadn't watched them get engaged, so it wouldn't be fair for them to horn in on us."

Peggy became very serious. "Joe, my Great Aunt Mattie *loathed* Ziggy Mulholland." There. She had voiced the crux of her worries.

"Loathed him? Not...ex-act-ly," Joe replied, looking down at her as all the noisy people moved slowly in a mass around them, ignoring the two lovers. "My Great Uncle Ziggy was in a long decline before he died, and he told me all about Mattie and him.

"You see, your Great Aunt Mattie was a preliberation liberated woman, with her own means, and she refused to marry Ziggy. They had the most torrid, romantic, wild, lifelong affair of all time."

Surprise turned Peggy rigid in Joe's arms. "She hated him!"

"Ummmm." His hands soothed her, convincing her to relax again. "Well, perhaps. Now and then," he conceded. "People who love that violently fight that violently, too." His voice was gentle. "Uncle Ziggy said every time she flew into a snit over him and left him 'forever' she came down to San Antonio for refuge in the bosom of her family."

"And she raged to me about men."

"Ah," said Joe in understanding.

"But it was only a temporary alienation?"

"How often was she in San Antonio and raging?"

"Not very often," Peggy replied thoughtfully.

"All the rest of the time, she and Ziggy were giggling and making love...like I want to do with you."

"That's just sex." She invited elaboration.

"It's a lifetime commitment. You came into that lobby and I knew you right away from the pictures that I saw—"

"What pictures?"

"Taken at Padre Island a couple of years ago. That flesh-colored bikini about blew my head off."

"Who took those?" she gasped.

"One of the members of the Men's Club," Joe explained. "But pictures—as good as those were—can't hold a candle to the real Margaret Dillon! You walked into that lobby with that sulky mouth and those big eyes and that walk. My God. It had to be you, but until I saw your actual driver's license I couldn't believe my luck. You really were Margaret Indiana Dillon. I thought you might be a very expensive call girl."

"Call girl?" she asked indignantly.

"Going into a hotel at midday without luggage, all duked up in a navy-blue suit and coming out in that gorgeous, eye-catching, purple suit..."

"Gorgeous purple...?" Her voice faltered.

"All really expensive call girls look like elementary education teachers," he assured her earnestly.

"Just how would you know that?"

"I've heard it all my life. When my daddy taught me to always turn my watch clockwise, and never counter-clockwise, he also told me there are expensive call girls that disguise themselves very cleverly as elementary education teachers, and when a nice young boy sees a beautiful girl who is luscious and sweet, and looks like an el ed teacher, he has to be very careful he isn't drawn into her net and...ruined."

"Ruined?" she echoed flatly.

"Right," Joe said, with conviction covering his humor nicely. "He'll become ensnared, depraved, thinking only of love—and he's...lost." He studied her. "*You* look like an el ed teacher."

"I am one."

"And I'm lost." He sighed, accepting his fate.

"So..." She leaned her head back and half closed her eyes as she smiled a small, seductive smile. "So you were terrified of me. I never suspected for a minute."

"You weren't supposed to. My daddy told me about that, too. 'Pretend you aren't scared, Joseph,' he said. 'Pretend you're not scared or uncertain or terrified of losing her, or she just might get away.'"

"Why me? Of all the women in the world, why me?"

"I've given that considerable thought," he informed her as they were again pressed closely by the crowd. "And I'm damned if I know. I'd say to myself, 'Joseph—' I always call myself Joseph since my daddy does and it sounds like it's more serious that way. So I said to myself, 'Joseph, why Margaret Indiana Dillon of all the women in the world? Just because she's gorgeous and interesting and sweet, why her?' And I would ponder on it.

"I finally decided you supplied that answer yourself when I discovered you aren't frigid with me. You're a one-man woman, and obviously I am that man. It's my fate. I can't fight it. I just have to submit. Let's go over to my place."

"Your place!" She still had her mouth open in astonishment at his "damned if I know," and she was indignantly charmed by his dissertation on the whys and wherefores of his attraction to her. "Your place? I know! You've quit smoking and you need something to do with your hands." She smiled slightly, waiting for whatever he would reply to that.

"I lied. I never have smoked. I thought if I told you I was quitting it would catch your sympathy and you'd be sweet to me. Everybody knows how hard it is to quit...."

"How sneaky you are!"

"I'd try anything to catch your attention, since I know I'm the only man you could possibly love and without me you'd have a bleak, loveless life. Let's go to my place. We can find a calendar and figure out when we're getting married."

"I've only known you for four days! That's not long enough for such a commitment."

"Can't you recognize the inevitable?" He frowned at her. "Any woman who could wear that purple suit with such flair couldn't possibly be a stickler for convention." His eyes were drawn to the butterfly, but he didn't mention it.

"Honey," he said with patience, "we were together for four twenty-four-hour periods. Any date lasts, say, two to four hours. If we had been dating, with the dates strung out over days instead of concentrated that way, we'd have had at least thirty dates—or *more*! That would equal several months of heavy dating.

"We know we get along very well. I find you fascinating. You only snore little ladylike snores." He ignored her ladylike snort of objection. "And our senses of humor match just the same nice interesting way our bodies match. The way I have it figured, we'll court publicly for a reasonable length of time so everyone else can adjust to the idea and not be shocked over the apparent suddenness of our marriage.

"I want to marry you, my love. I love you to the heights and depths my soul can reach. I want to live with you and be your love."

"Oh, Joe."

He kissed her beautifully, then said huskily, "Let's go to my place."

"And you can make love to me," she guessed.

"What a good idea!"

"Well, I won't. I did slip that one time, but you'll just have to wait. If I gave out...samples to every man who said he'd marry me, I could qualify as that el ed call girl."

"Lots of guys after you, huh? No wonder."

"There have been several very earnest ones."

"Anyone I know?"

"You."

"You mean I've been that obvious?"

"That first morning when you said for me to get back in bed."

"Too obvious?" he inquired.

"Yes."

"Why, Margaret Indiana Dillon—soon to be Margaret Indiana Dillon Mulholland—I'll bet you aren't as reluctant as you pretend to be. You've been after my body ever since you first laid eyes on me, and you've just been leading me on, so I would think I was the one who was chasing you, but all this time it's been *you* chasing *me*!"

"Oh, shut up," she told him mildly.

"You've got to quit saying 'shut up' and learn to say 'hush' or all our children will be yelling shut up and sounding nasty when they could be yelling hush and not sounding nearly so ornery."

"Hush."

"That's my girl." His voice was low, and she could feel the vibrations from his chest against hers. "My woman," he corrected himself, and there was a sexual intensity in his declaration.

"Yes." She not only agreed she was his, she agreed she would marry him, accepting him completely there in that mad, wonderful, colorful, friendly place.

He kissed her—a lovely, tender kiss—holding her to him with rigidly controlled arms. Then he said, "You agreed. You said 'yes.' You're committed forever, for all your life and all through time. Under those circumstances I'll have to do the honorable thing and marry you."

"Not if you don't want to. You don't have to do anything of the kind." She was sassily confident as she smiled at him.

"Ah, but I want you exclusively."

She watched him for a minute; then her smile deepened. "If you intend to get what you want, I guess you will have to marry me."

"That's what I figured." And he too smiled. "Are you back to your frigid, normal self? Will I have to go to all that trouble to try to thaw you out again?"

"I...don't...believe so. I always thought I was un-thawable, but on the elevator when I first saw you standing there—"

"Now how could you have seen me? I took off my hat with great care so that you *wouldn't* see me."

"You did that deliberately?"

"Of course. We couldn't have you recognizing me from the hotel when we captured you out on the highway. You'd have smelled a rat, wouldn't you?"

To "smell the rat" she tilted her head, with its butterfly, and delicately sniffed along his jaw and throat. She did it very erotically.

He licked his lips, the sheen of sexual sweat beginning to bead on his forehead and upper lip. He pulled his head back to study her. "This guy...the one who said you were cold..."

"Frigid," she corrected.

"Frigid," Joe acknowledged. "Was he physically repulsive? A revolting personality? Didn't he bathe? What was his trouble?"

"Him? The trouble with him?"

"It sure as hell couldn't have been you! You're about the hottest woman I've ever had my hands on."

"Just how many women have you had your hands on?"

"Uh...well...you see..." And then he just laughed. "Well, I can't remember a single, solitary one—other than you. And since I'm so new at this love business, it'd be very nice if you could show me again just how unfrigid you are, now that I'm going to marry you and all. You could give me a nice, squishy kiss for starters."

"I don't think I should. Not here."

"Why not? Nobody's paying us any mind at all."

"When you kiss me...I get a little wild inside."

"Do you really? How wild?"

She blushed and looked down. "Very wild."

"Show me."

"I don't dare. Not here." She looked around and found that they were being ignored by the laughing, noisy crowd. She looked back up at him. "If you kissed me seriously, we would turn out to be such a spectacle that we'd be sensational, and then every gathering would want us to perform and it'd be a nuisance. What if we'd quarreled on a big night and didn't want to?"

"I can see the problem. We could go to my place and no one would notice us. First, though, my parents are waiting for me to bring you by so they can meet you. So we have to go there.

"Mother remembers she's met your family and you somewhere along the way, but she isn't sure she recalls you exactly. So we have to go see them first. Then we can go to my place and make love."

"What's wrong with the pickup? It served very well the first time."

"It shouldn't have been in the pickup. You didn't give me enough time to plan so that it could be lovely for you. It should have been in a rose bower."

"I have rose fever."

"I have Peggy fever."

"No. I'm allergic to roses," she explained.

"I think I'm allergic to you. You get near me and I get all nervous, and twitchy, and sweaty. I swell up and can't breath right...."

"I wouldn't have run away if you hadn't taken the moccasins," she confessed.

"The moccasins?" Since he was thinking about why he was twitchy and sweating, he had to bring his mind back to figure out what in the world she was talking about. "What about the moccasins?"

"When I woke up and found you'd taken them with you so I couldn't escape, I got mad and decided to—"

"I took them into town so I could buy you a better pair of shoes. I needed the size."

"Oh, Joe." A toothbrush and then shoes!

"Come on. Let's go. Let's get the visit to my folks out of the way so we can get down to the real business of the evening."

"I know: making love." She sighed falsely over the inevitable.

"No, no, no, no," he chided. "Getting married!"

"We're getting married tonight?" She pulled back a little in order to look at him.

"Deciding *when*." He turned her and began to edge them through the mob, holding her hand tightly as he led the way, making a path for her through the crush of people.

"How can I plan something so serious as marriage when I don't know anything about you? Really! I don't even know how you chipped your tooth!"

"Oh, that. It happened when I was pitched off that...*precious* horse a couple of weeks ago. I'm going to have the tooth capped next week."

"Oh, no!" she protested in real dismay. "I wish you wouldn't."

"Why not?" He turned and looked back at her over his shoulder in surprise.

"I think...well...I *like* it."

"You do?" He acted doubtful.

"It's...erotic."

"*All right!* What would happen if I chipped it a little more?"

"Heaven only knows."

He laughed as he led her past the hors d'oeuvres table near the French doors, and he said to her over his shoulder, "Come along. I'll get a hammer and chisel."

She laughed too as they went out the doors and into the night.

Henry turned away from the table and looked after the disappearing couple. He asked in a puzzled voice, "A hammer and chisel? Why would Joe want a hammer and chisel?"

And beside him Francine explained smoothly, "Well, she *is* twenty-two and still a virgin."

Henry smiled down at her and replied, "So are you, but I'm going to tamper with you."

"Tampa?" Francine laughed as she fell in with the old joke. "Why go to Florida?"

"We'll go there on our honeymoon. It'll be fun."

READERS' COMMENTS ON SILHOUETTE DESIRES

"Thank you for Silhouette Desires. They are the best thing that has happened to the bookshelves in a long time."

—V.W.*, Knoxville, TN

"Silhouette Desires—wonderful, fantastic—the best romance around."

—H.T.*, Margate, N.J.

"As a writer as well as a reader of romantic fiction, I found DESIREs most refreshingly realistic—and definitely as magical as the love captured on their pages."

—C.M.*, Silver Lake, N.Y.

"I just wanted to let you know how very much I enjoy your Silhouette Desire books. I read other romances, and I must say your books rate up at the top of the list."

—C.N.*, Anaheim, CA

"Desires are number one. I especially enjoy the endings because they just don't leave you with a kiss or embrace; they finish the story. Thank you for giving me such reading pleasure."

—M.S.*, Sandford, FL

*names available on request

AMERICAN TRIBUTE

Where a man's dreams count for more than his parentage...

Look for these upcoming titles under the Special Edition American Tribute banner.

LOVE'S HAUNTING REFRAIN
Ada Steward #289—February 1986
For thirty years a deep dark secret kept them apart—King Stockton made his millions while his wife, Amelia, held everything together. Now could they tell their secret, could they admit their love?

THIS LONG WINTER PAST
Jeanne Stephens #295—March 1986
Detective Cody Wakefield checked out Assistant District Attorney Liann McDowell, but only in his leisure time. For it was the danger of Cody's job that caused Liann to shy away.

Silhouette Special Edition

AMERICAN TRIBUTE

AMERICAN TRIBUTE

RIGHT BEHIND THE RAIN
Elaine Camp #301—April 1986
The difficulty of coping with her brother's
death brought reporter Raleigh Torrence
to the office of Evan Younger, a police
psychologist. He helped her to deal with
her feelings and emotions, including love.

CHEROKEE FIRE
Gena Dalton #307—May 1986
It was Sabrina Dante's silver spoon that
Cherokee cowboy Jarod Redfeather couldn't
trust. The two lovers came from opposite
worlds, but Jarod's Indian heritage taught
them to overcome their differences.

NOBODY'S FOOL
Renee Roszel #313—June 1986
Everyone bet that Martin Dante and Cara
Torrence would get together. But Martin
wasn't putting any money down, and Cara
was out to prove that she was nobody's fool.

MISTY MORNINGS, MAGIC NIGHTS
Ada Steward #319—July 1986
The last thing Carole Stockton wanted was to
fall in love with another politician, especially
Donnelly Wakefield. But under a blanket of
secrecy, far from the campaign spotlights,
their love became a powerful force.

Silhouette Desire

COMING NEXT MONTH

A MUCH NEEDED HOLIDAY—Joan Hohl
Neither Kate nor Trace had believed in holiday magic until they
were brought together during the Christmas rush and discovered
the joy of the season together.

MOONLIGHT SERENADE—Laurel Evans
A small-town radio jazz program was just Emma's speed—until
New York executive Simon Eliot tried to get her to shift gears and
join him in the fast lane.

HERO AT LARGE—Aimée Martel
Writing about the Air Force Pararescue School was a difficult task,
and with Commandant Bob Logan watching her every move,
Leslie had a hard time keeping her mind on her work.

TEACHER'S PET—Ariel Berk
Cecily was a teacher who felt deeply about the value of an
education. Nick had achieved success using his wits. Despite their
differences could they learn the lesson of love?

HOOK, LINE AND SINKER—Elaine Camp
Roxie had caught herself an interview with expert angler
Sonny Austin by telling him she was a fishing pro. Now she was on
the hook to make good her claim.

LOVE BY PROXY—Diana Palmer
Amelia's debut as a belly dancer was less than auspicious. Rather
than dazzling her surprised audience with her jingling bangles, she
wound up losing her job, her head and her heart.
